CLAN OF THE BIGFOOT

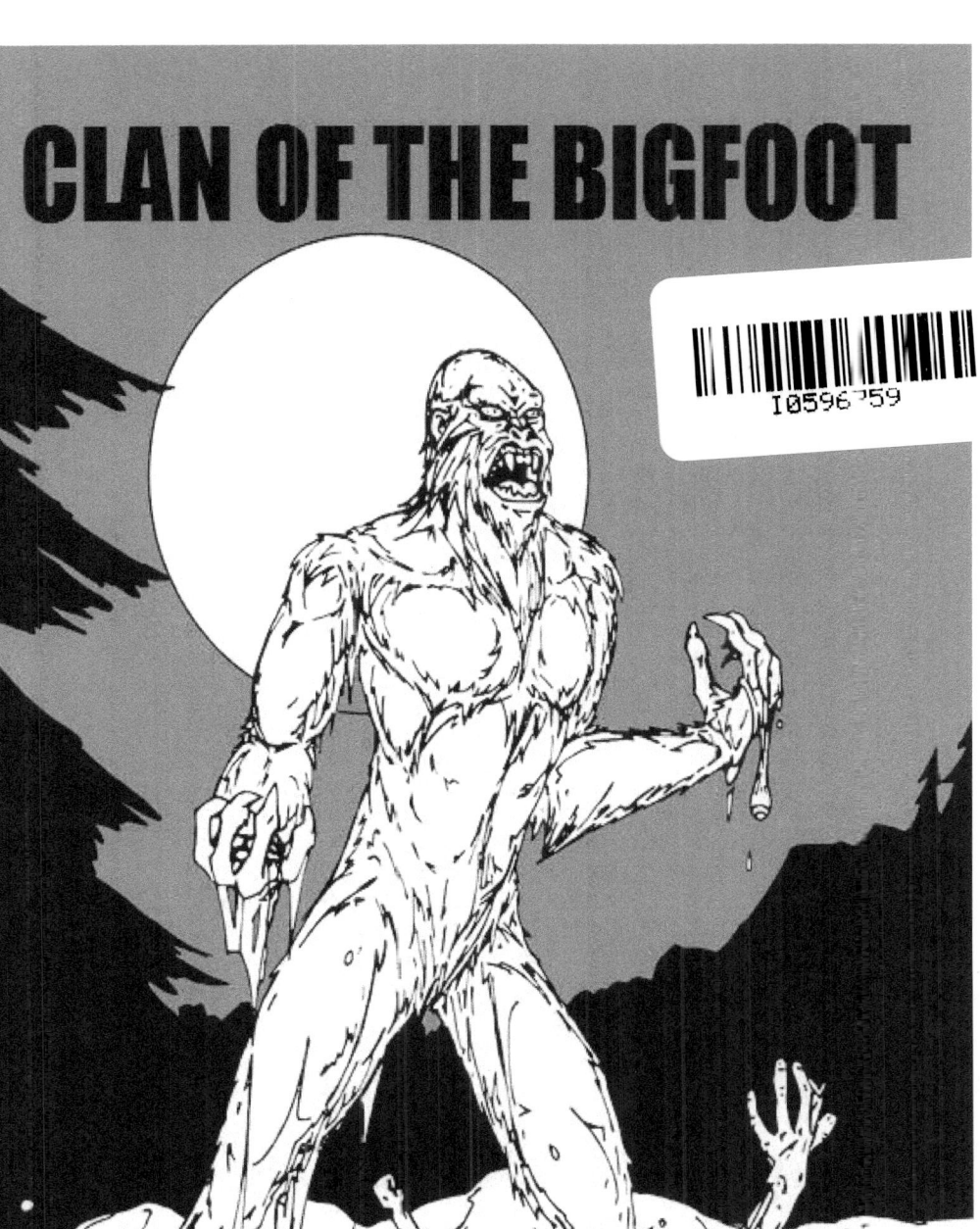

ANTHONY GIANGREGORIO

CLAN OF THE BIGFOOT

ANTHONY GIANGREGORIO

INTRODUCTION
BY
ERIC S. BROWN

THE RETURN OF BIGFOOT

Bigfoot horror has been a large part of the B movie world for decades. Classic films about the creature such as The Legend of Boggy Creek still have massive cult followings and new Bigfoot films are constantly being made. Some are well done and awesome like Sasquatch Mountain, some are tongue in cheek like Abominable, and some like the simply titled Bigfoot (2010) are barely able to be endured thanks to budget limitations.

Even Boggy Creek itself is being remade and the new version is supposedly set to hit DVD sometime in 2011. Despite all the movies and Bigfoot's cult following, there has never been much in the way of Bigfoot novels or novellas. For whatever reason, Bigfoot, not so unlike zombies before John Skipp and Craig Spector's Book of the Dead, hasn't really been explored in the world of literature. Trust me, I have searched the web over for books that give the monster his due and make him relevant to contemporary horror culture. This astounding lack of Bigfoot fiction led me to write my own trilogy on the subject. As a fan, I wanted to see Bigfoot come out of the woods and kick some major butt, zombie apocalypse style. I wanted to give a monster I loved as a child some teeth again and make us terrified to go into the woods alone.

Bigfoot horror has been out of the limelight for so long it's like the genre is brand new all over again. In a world where it seems everything has been done before, Bigfoot gives a horror writer a fresh and powerful new sub-genre to explore. It's my personal hope that we'll see a growing movement of Crypto-Horror in the small press and beyond. I know TOR Publishing already has plans to release a Bigfoot novel from James Robert Smith this year and hopefully they'll be far from the only major publisher to do so. If you're holding this book in your hands, you likely agree with me. I can tell you, you will not be disappointed. Anthony Giangregorio is a writer who does not hold back his punches. He's a master story-teller with the heart of a fan. His work in the zombie genre speaks volumes.

The Clan of the Bigfoot is a work that will likely stand as one of the best this new genre has to offer in its infancy and be remembered as one that truly stood out among its peers. Lock the doors, turn on all the lights, and keep a bloody big gun beside your chair...

Because the monsters are coming.

PART ONE

THE CABIN

"I don't believe it. We're lost, aren't we?" Karen said from the passenger seat as she stared at the map spread out before her. The overhead visor light was on so she could see better, the daylight fading fast.

"We're not lost, the cabin is around here somewhere," Michael replied as he maneuvered the car past a sharp bend in the road.

Over two hours had passed since the road changed from asphalt to gravel, and then to sodden dirt. The rains had carved deep grooves into the road, causing the car to jump on its shocks like Michael had decided to take them offroading.

The fading sunlight tried to break through the canopy of tree branches but failed miserably. All around, everything was waterlogged, as if God Himself had decided this part of the world needed a good dousing.

The rain pummeled the car like a living thing, small metallic hammering, a staccato of nature at its worse.

"We need to turn around," Karen said as she tossed the map into the back seat where some of their supplies were. "The cabin isn't on this road. You need to turn around before you get us so lost we never find our way out." She stared out through the front windshield at the forbidding woods as dusk descended fast.

The forest was so beautiful in the daylight. Why was it that when the sun went down it became so frightening?

She assumed it was something primal, something that harked back to when man first crawled from the muck and went out into the darkness.

She caught movement out of the corner of her eye and she gasped in surprise, then squinted to try to catch what had grabbed her attention in the gloom. Her head swiveled as the car passed by the spot she was watching, but the shadow didn't reappear. She shrugged, deciding it must have been a trick of the fading light.

"We can't turn around, dear," Michael said, saying the word *dear* sarcastically. "There's no place I can manage it. The trees grow right up to the edge of the road, and even if I still tried, the shoulder's muddy. This isn't a truck, you know, we'll get stuck and if that happens we'll end up walking." He turned to look at her. "Do *you* want to walk in this rain in the middle of nowhere?"

"Oh, is that what you call what we're on, a road?" she added in a sarcastic tone of her own as she crossed her arms over her chest. Her dark brown hair, just past her shoulders, was trapped between her arms and body.

He continued to look away from the road long enough to stare her down. He knew in a marriage sometimes it was the one who held his gaze the longest that won the argument.

"Be nice, this isn't my fault," he said calmly.

She had been prepared to snap at him, expecting him to do the same, but when he ended up talking calmly, it threw her off.

"Oh, I...I know that, Michael, it's just...we're getting deeper into the woods, who knows what's out here. We need to turn back and get directions. What if we break down?"

He nodded at her words, taking them in. "Yeah, I was thinking the same thing." He pointed to his cell phone on the dashboard, the cord to the cigarette lighter keeping it charged. "Check that, will you? Do we even have a signal out here?"

She did as he asked and a second later shook her head. "Nope, no signal, there's no bars at all."

"Great, that's what I was afraid of." He shrugged slightly and sighed. "Look, Karen, I'm pretty sure we're on the right road. All we need to do is follow it till we either reach the cabin or till it ends. Then I can turn around and we can go back."

"This was a mistake," she said and wrapped her arms around herself protectively. "We shouldn't have come out here. We're city people, camping isn't our thing. I should be home in bed right now with a drink and the TV on, all snuggled up in a warm blanket. I don't know why I let you talk me into this."

"Oh, please," he said. "I used to go camping all the time when I was a kid. My uncle left me this cabin more than two years ago and I want to use it at least once before I die."

"Yes, you did go camping, but that was with your father when you were eleven. He did everything for you, too, you didn't have to do a thing."

"Maybe, but I still remember enough so we can have some fun. Besides, it's not like we're sleeping outside or anything. The cabin is like a small house, only with the one room."

"Yeah, and no bathroom. I swear, Michael, I never in my life imagined I would have to poop in a hole. It's 2011 for Christ's sake."

"Well, either way, we need to find it first. We must be miles from the highway by now. My uncle built the cabin out here for a reason. He wanted to get as far away from civilization as he could, to really feel like he was all alone in the world. I swear, some of us in the family thought one day he would simply pack up and go live in a cave for the rest of his life. A true hermit in every sense. I told you that for his entire life he never had a telephone, right?"

She nodded. "Yes, many times. I have to admit, that is something else. In this world to go your entire life without even a phone." She smiled inwardly. "I could never live without a cell phone, it's a part of me now." She looked out at the trees, the branches swaying back and forth with the wind. It was a truly brutal day and with darkness falling, the night seemed no better. She wished they were at the cabin right now instead of traveling on a deserted road. "How far in the woods do you think we are now?"

"Well, we've been driving for hours, so I'd say twenty miles easy. I did tell you it was in the middle of nowhere," he replied.

She turned to him then, her eyes wide with surprise. "You mean to tell me we're more than twenty miles deep in the woods with no cell service in the middle of the pouring rain, and no idea where

12

the cabin is? Is that what you're telling me?" Her face was red as she became more upset.

"Well, yeah, I guess so. But when you put it that way I guess it does sound pretty bad." He chuckled a little as he swung around another dip in the road. "Come on, Karen, this isn't the movies. There's no man with a leather mask and a chainsaw chasing us or monsters that want to eat us for lunch, all of them out there watching us. There's no banjos playing haunting lyrics, no inbred hillbillies that have daughters with fathers that are their brothers, too. That's just the stuff of Hollywood to make people scared and sell tickets. We're perfectly safe. And besides," he patted his jacket, "I have my .38 if someone's stupid enough to mess with us."

She shook her head, her dark tresses caressing her cheeks. "I don't know, Michael. We haven't seen any signs of civilization for hours. For all we know, we're the only ones out here and the cabin is on the other side of the woods."

"Yeah, maybe," he replied and concentrated on the road, realizing he hadn't been doing a very good job of it.

With the car jumping and bucking through the large puddles like a wild bronco, they drove deeper into the dense forest, the darkness consuming their world an inch at a time.

"You know, it's funny…" Michael said as he fought the wheel, the car bouncing over yet another bad dip in the road.

13

Karen waited for him to continue. When he didn't, she frowned. "What's funny?" she prodded, her arms crossed over her chest again. She was cold and no matter how high the heat was she felt a chill.

He shrugged slightly, something he did often when he was considering something. "Well, it's just that we're so far in the woods now, you know? I mean, this is the kind of place you'd find Bigfoot skulking around between the trees."

"Bigfoot? Oh, Michael, don't be silly. Besides, Bigfoot has had sightings only in the northwest, we're in the east."

He looked at her, his left eyebrow rising in curiosity. "And how in the world do you even know that?"

She shrugged, brushing her hair from her face. "I just do. I read and watch TV, too, you know."

He reached out and cupped her chin in his hand, rubbing her cheek with his thumb. It was times like this when he was reminded of just how much he loved her. It was when she showed something about herself he didn't know was there. Even after almost ten years of marriage, she could still surprise him.

It was as he was looking at her, his eyes off the road again, that something darted out of the treeline to end up in the path of the car.

Karen was the first to see the shadowy figure caught in the headlights. She screamed, "Michael, lookout!" and slammed her hands onto the dashboard.

Michael's gaze went back to the road and his eyes went wide when he saw something before him. He also knew there would be no time to stop before connecting with the shape.

Still he tried. His foot smashed the brake pedal to the floorboard, and the tires locked up and began to slide in the mud.

Michael had just enough time to see two small eyes reflecting— seeming to glow— in the headlights, and then the car made contact with the figure while at the same time the front tire dropped into a deep pothole. There was a thud and then silence, other than the rain pattering on the car, *tick, tick, tick,* relentlessly.

The vehicle came to a halt so hard and fast that both of them were thrown forward. Neither was wearing a seatbelt, deciding in the middle of nowhere it wasn't needed, and with the new laws demanding they wear one in the city, they both felt like little rebels by unbuckling them as soon as they reached the mountain pass. But now the lack of seatbelts was a detraction as both of them were tossed around the car like rag dolls from the sudden halt.

Karen's head struck the windshield and she was lifted a foot off her seat, as Michael cried out in pain, the steering wheel digging deep into his upper chest. He felt bolts of pain shoot through his body and he knew immediately he might have cracked a rib.

The car lurched forward as the brakes locked up and the left front tire sank a foot into the water-filled hole, then it rocked back as the two passengers were slammed back against their seats.

There was a small blood spot on the windshield where Karen's head had connected with the glass, her body slumped forward in the seat, unconscious.

Michael sucked in a breath of air, trying to fight the pain in his chest, but his body was slipping into shock, and before he could stop himself, he felt the world going dark.

He reached out and tried to touch Karen, wanting to see if she was all right, but before he could, his arm dropped to the seat and he slipped into oblivion.

Outside, the shape lay still before the car, the rain pounding down harder than ever.

There was a tapping sound filling his dream as Michael finally came back to full wakefulness.

For a brief second, he thought he was blind. His eyes were open but he couldn't see a thing. Looking left and right, the tapping grew louder. It was coming from above him, and as he reached out and felt the switch for the window, he pressed the button, the window rolling down.

Immediately he was splashed with water and he realized the noise was rain hitting the roof and hood of the car; he raised the window.

The car had stalled after hitting the shape and pothole. He looked to the dash and could see the dim glow of the numbers and letters. Reaching out, he turned on the dome light and was blinded by the glare until his eyes could focus again.

Then he gasped in shock to see Karen slumped in her seat, her head resting against the passenger window, her mouth parted slightly, drool wetting her chin.

"Oh God, Karen? Are you all right, oh God, please say something," he whispered as he leaned over and pulled her to him. She groaned slightly and he said a silent prayer, grateful she was alive. He felt her head, and when his hand came away with blood on it, he gasped again. When he inspected her scalp, he found a small cut on the top of her forehead where her head had whacked the windshield.

She groaned again and her eyes fluttered open. "Ohhhh, what the hell happened?"

"I don't know, I think we hit something," Michael said as he tried to clear his still foggy mind. All the windows were covered with condensation and he couldn't see out any of them.

"Hit something? We're in the middle of the forest. How the hell did you manage that?"

"Like I just said, I don't know. I think it was a deer or something. It darted out from between the trees. I couldn't stop. Remember? You yelled and then I hit the brakes? Are you hurt? I mean, other than that cut on your head?"

She took stock of herself, groaning as she sat up, but after a minute passed in silence, Karen knew she was fine, only a splitting headache the result of the crash.

"I'm okay, just a bad headache. How 'bout you?"

Michael winced slightly in the glow of the dome light. "My chest hurts a little, but I'll live."

She smiled wanly. "Want me to kiss the boo-boo and make it all better?"

"Ha, ha, I really don't think now is the time for that," he replied as he shifted in his seat, wincing from the pain in his chest.

He put the car into park, the engine having stalled, and now he tried to start it again. The motor started right up, but as he tried to move the car, it wouldn't budge. He could feel the engine wanting to push the car along but the vehicle felt like it was dragging or like it had a flat. He knew there was only one thing to do.

Turning off the engine, but leaving the headlights on, he reached into the backseat for his jacket and a flashlight as Karen watched silently.

She rubbed at her window, the condensation coming away, but she couldn't see a thing. It was pitch black outside on the road and the surrounding woods, the rain only adding to the sense of utter loneliness.

"How long was I out?" she wondered aloud, but Michael thought she was speaking to him.

"I don't know, maybe an hour I guess. I was out, too. We both took a beating. Guess that's what we get for not wearing our seatbelts, huh?"

Her reply was a soft grunt. She didn't need to hear a lecture about auto safety. He opened his door and was about to get out when she grabbed his arm and asked, "Wait, where're you going?"

"I have to see what's wrong with the car, Karen."

"But it's raining out, you'll get soaked."

He grinned at her. "Karen, it's only rain, I'll be fine. Now you stay here and try to rest, I'll be right back."

"You be careful," she told him and he nodded while pushing the door open and stepping out.

As soon as his foot came down, it was swallowed by a six inch puddle and he felt the cold water seep into his hiking boot. Cursing silently, he ignored it and slammed the door closed to keep the inside of the car dry. He turned on the flashlight and shrugged into his jacket, all the while moving to the front of the vehicle.

The headlights barely helped push back the night, the rain and fog from the moisture in the air bringing visibility down to nothing. He managed to make it to the front bumper without falling on his face.

Once there, he flashed the light on the tires, and after checking the driver's side and seeing all was well, he checked the right tire to see it was fine as well, though it seemed to be in a deep pothole, the water level even with the center cap of the hubcap.

As he spun around to look at the road ahead, the beam of the flashlight illuminated a shape on the shoulder of the road about ten feet away, just out of reach of the headlights.

Walking away from the car, Michael leaned over what looked like a small animal. Gingerly touching it, he found it was very dead, the fur matted with mud and blood so thick even the rain couldn't wash it away.

A quick guess told him he'd hit a baby grizzly bear. Knowing the pelt was valuable, he put the flashlight in his pocket, scooped up the bear in his arms, and carried it back to the car. After popping the trunk, he placed the carcass in with the camping supplies.

Slamming the trunk closed, he ran back to the driver's door to get inside when a flash of lightning lit up the sky. His eyes were looking straight ahead, and as the night turned into day for a brief second, he spotted a one foot wide sign lying sideways on the ground at the treeline. He knew the sign well and saw that it had fallen off the tree it was mounted to.

He opened the door and got into the car, glad to be out of the rain again. With his hair matted to his head and water dripping down his sodden face, he smiled at Karen. "You won't believe what I found," he said with excitement.

She had played this game with him before and with her splitting headache was in no mood for guessing games. "Just tell me, please. Is the car okay?"

"Yes, the car's fine, but it looks like we hit a baby grizzly bear."

She frowned. "Is that what you put in the trunk? Why would you do that? I want it out of there right now."

He shook his head, adamant. "No way, Karen. That pelt will make an awesome rug, it stays." He pointed to the front of the car.

"And I know where we are. The cabin is about two miles away. I saw a marker when that lightning flashed."

Her eyes lit up with relief, the bear carcass forgotten. "You mean we're not lost?"

He laughed at her relief. "No, honey, we're not lost. We'll be at the cabin in a few minutes, I promise.

He started the engine again and put the car in reverse. After the tire slipped for a few seconds, it finally freed itself of the pothole with a wet squelch of reverse suction. Michael made a wide berth around the pothole, as he couldn't see it under the water that had filled it.

With both of them in a better mood, now knowing they were safe and their destination imminent, they continued on their journey.

As the car drove onward, blood from the dead carcass pooled in the trunk to then seep out of the drain holes in the floorboard.

Each drop landed in the rain-soaked earth to be diluted, but to a sensitive nose, it would still be there when the rainstorm finally abated, a trail of breadcrumbs for any who wanted to follow it.

* * *

Twenty minutes later, Michael pulled into the long driveway leading to the cabin. He drove up the winding drive and finally came to the cabin itself. Despite knowing where he was going, he had taken two wrong turns, thanks to the road looking vastly different in the dark, the rain obscuring anything more than a few feet away.

The cabin was nestled amidst the surrounding trees, some no more than six feet from the foundation. Knee high grass surrounded it on all three sides, attesting to the last time someone had been on the grounds and maintained it.

The saying, 'the middle of nowhere' was very apt in a description of the cabin's location.

"Stay here and I'll go unlock the front door," he told Karen, who only nodded in reply. The blood had dried in her hair and small flakes fell onto the seat as she moved her head.

Michael jumped out of the car and dashed the fifteen feet to the front door. After digging in his pocket for a few seconds, he came out with a single key with a worn, white, paper tag tied to it. Sliding it into the lock, the door opened easily. He waved to Karen to come on and she did, also running to the door, only she kept going until she was inside.

"I'll get our gear," he said and ran back out into the rain.

Karen looked around the cabin for the first time, the interior mostly shadows layered upon more shadows. As she turned to her right, she jumped, startled, but then lightning flashed and she saw what she thought was a wild animal was in reality a stuffed moose head mounted to the wall.

The glass eyes reflected the ambient light, making her feel they were following her as she moved about the room.

She chided herself for being such a 'girl' and willed herself to be strong. The room was sparsely decorated, only the bare necessities for the true wilderness buff. There was a made, full-size bed in the far corner with a thin layer of dust on its surface. Next to it were a simple wooden chair, and a small nightstand.

The middle of the room had a couch made out of arm-thick logs and a fireplace on the back wall. In the corner, across from the bed, was a three foot table and three more wooden chairs. There was no kitchen, only a counter where a few old boxes of dried goods sat, a trail of mouse turds leading away from them.

There were no other doors beside the front door and only two windows, and she knew to go to the bathroom, an outhouse was located at the rear of the building. When Michael had told her that bit of information back at their home in the city, she had smiled sweetly, and when he'd looked away to deal with their camping gear, she had rolled her eyes, wondering what she was getting herself into.

"Wonderful," she said to herself. "All the comforts of home and then some. Martha Stewart, eat your heart out."

Footsteps sounded behind her and she turned to see Michael standing at the door, dripping water on the floor, also tracking mud inside. He was holding the bear carcass in his hands, blood dripping onto the floor to mix with the water and mud.

"What are you doing with *that*?" she asked in a disgusted voice.

"I'm bringing it inside the cabin. What's it look like?" he replied.

"I don't want that thing in here. Leave it outside."

He shook his head. "I can't. If I leave it outside, the animals will be attracted to it. It'll end up being dragged away."

"Then leave it in the trunk."

"No way. I can't unpack the supplies if the body's in there, now can I? Besides, it's all wet and it needs to dry out or it'll stink, and that won't happen in the trunk."

She rolled her eyes, his thinking irrational, but she was simply too tired to argue with him.

"Fine, but I don't want it anywhere near me."

"No problem." He walked across the cabin and put the carcass down near the fireplace. She glanced at it, seeing nothing but a mud-covered, bloody carcass of what she guessed was a bear cub. Not that she would have known if Michael hadn't told her.

She was a city girl and other than what she saw on television and at the zoo, the most bizarre animal she had ever seen was a ferret her neighbor had owned for a while until the little critter had escaped one day when the back door was left open.

There was a blanket on the back of the couch and Michael took it off and draped it over the carcass. "There, that'll do for now. I'll gut it and clean it later."

She swallowed hard. "You mean you're going to…"

He nodded. "Yup, have to or it'll rot from the inside out. Don't worry, I'll do it outside tomorrow. Then I can wash the pelt and let it cure till we leave. My dad taught me how, though I have to admit this will be my first time doing it myself."

24

CLAN OF THE BIGFOOT

"Ugh, spare me the details," she said, too tired from the night's ordeal to want to hear it. She went to lie down on the couch. "We need a fire."

"I'll do it in a second, you lay down and rest," he told her and went back outside to get the supplies.

A few minutes later, after bringing in most of the gear, he began prepping the fire. The rain was tapering off finally, but the air was still heavy with moisture.

There was a small stack of firewood inside the cabin and Michael said a silent thank you that someone had taken the time to put them there years ago. Anything outside was soaked to its core, and if not for the dry wood, he might have had to take a chair apart for fuel.

A little later, with oil lamps burning, a warm fire caressing them both, and full bellies from their canned goods, the young couple drifted off to sleep in the bed with their clothes on. Both were too tired to do anything more than wash up, and even that had been halfhearted.

While they slept, the carcass under the blanket shifted slightly as it settled, and a paw flopped out from under the blanket. Though similar at first glance to a grizzly bear, this paw was slightly different. The claws were three sizes larger and the end of the paw looked distinctly human, the protuberances of five digits apparent. Under the mud caking the fur was a more pronounced skeleton, much like what would have been found in a Neanderthal or perhaps a Cro-Magnon man.

And the fur itself though a pelt, on closer examination resembled coarse human hair rather than animal.

The blood under the carcass had begun to dry but still the redolence of iron hung heavy in the cabin, seeping through the cracks in the windows to permeate the outside air.

Any animal with a keen sense of smell would be able to detect it and with the cessation of rain, only more so.

Michael was pulled from sleep by a banging sound. At first he didn't know what it was, but by the second *bang*, he knew something was going on; something was trying to get into the cabin.

It was loud, very loud and only his slumber had deadened it at first.

Sitting up, he reached out for his .38, which he had placed on the small nightstand. The gun had been brought for protection, not hunting, he when he'd packed it, he never imagined he would have to use it.

Another *bang* filled the cabin, causing him to jump.

Sliding out of bed and standing up, he glanced to the fireplace. It was nothing but glowing coals and the oil lamps had been doused hours ago. The cabin was all but in total darkness.

The dull illumination that filtered past the thin curtains on the two windows wasn't enough to see by, and the few items in the cabin were no more than blurry shapes, each barely indistinguishable from the other.

Another *bang* sounded on the cabin wall and he glanced at Karen, amazed she was still sleeping.

Walking over to one of the windows, he stopped and froze when he heard a mournful wail coming from outside. Part coyote and part moose, it was the strangest sound he'd ever heard.

He was about to turn and yell at Karen to get up, when the glass in the window exploded inward and a large shadow filled the entire frame.

Covering his face as glass shards pelted him, Michael screamed and fell to the floor. As he looked up at the window, expecting to see a grizzly bear or perhaps a rogue moose, his eyes went wide when he saw what seemed to be a giant hairy man, only this man was over seven feet tall with hair covering every part of his body. He knew then it couldn't be a man.

A long and hairy arm reached inside the cabin, swiping at him. Luckily, Michael was just out of reach. The arm was longer than a normal human's and the fingers on the hand were tipped with razor sharp claws. He didn't want to think what would happen if those claws found his flesh.

The hairy figure roared in anger at Michael, and as it did, Michael could see the sharp pointed teeth framed in the oval mouth.

If this was a man, it was an offshoot from humanity, some kind of missing link.

Though all this flooded Michael's mind instantly, what also suffused him was adrenalin. A scream ripped the air from behind and he glanced over his shoulder to see Karen sitting up in bed, her eyes wide in terror, her mouth still open after eliciting the scream.

In the back of his mind, Michael thought, *Well, at least she's up, too, and sees this. I'm not imagining it.*

The hairy figure kept swiping the air with its claws, but its torso was far too large to fit through the window. Michael stared in horror and fear for over thirty seconds until he realized he still had the .38 in his hand.

Raising it, he aimed the muzzle at the creature and fired.

It was a shaking hand that held the gun and the bullet only grazed the creature's arm. The hairy figure let out a yowl and immediately backed out of the window.

The walls of the cabin began to shake as the creature pounded on the wall again, and when the shadow went across the window, he fired again.

Michael didn't know how intelligent the creature was but it seemed to understand what a gun was and what it could do to it. With a few more seconds of pounding on the cabin, the beast turned and loped off into the forest, Michael hearing the crunching sounds of its heavy footfalls until it faded to silence.

"What the hell was that thing!" Karen screamed from the bed. Michael stood up, went to the window to peer into the night, and upon seeing nothing, went to Karen.

"I don't know. I have no idea at all. I want to say it was a grizzly bear but it looked nothing like one. It was almost human."

"I want to leave here, Michael. I want to leave here right fucking now!" she yelled and began to cry.

He hugged her tightly, trying to act brave but deep down he was terrified.

He shook his head. "We can leave in the morning, but I'll be honest with you, honey. If there's an animal out there like that, I don't want to be traveling through the woods in the dark, even in a car. The size of that thing could flip the car easily. Look, it'll be daylight in a few hours. We can leave then, I promise."

"No! I want to leave now, right now!" she cried.

"No, we can't. Like I just said, if it's still out there, I don't want to be trapped in the car. At least here we have four solid walls to protect us. In the car we'd be helpless. And what if the car got stuck in the mud again? We were lucky the last time that I got it out easily." He extricated himself from her. "Here, let me get the fire going again. Once there's more light in here you'll feel better. And besides..." He patted the gun again where he'd put it in his waistband. "I scared it off. It's probably miles away from here by now. I think I hit it, too, but I'm not sure."

They argued for a few more minutes but Karen finally relented, though she wasn't in full agreement.

"Well, I'm not sleeping for the rest of the night," she said. "I'm telling you that right now. And what about that window?"

Hunched over by the fireplace as he tried to restart the fire, Michael glanced at the open window. It wasn't cold outside and a warm wind was blowing into the cabin.

"It's fine for now," he told her. "Before we leave in the morning I'll see what I can do to cover it, then I can come back up next weekend to fix it right with the correct supplies." He walked over and joined her on the bed again, the fire already beginning to crackle anew.

He reached out and took her hand, rubbing the top of it with his thumb. "Karen, listen to me. We're perfectly safe here. Whatever that thing was, whatever just happened, it's all over now. I scared it off, it's long gone. It probably just wanted our food."

"Yes, that must be it, it just wanted our food. It must have been a bear you saw," she said, trying to convince herself. She nodded bashfully, a little embarrassed at her terror now that it was all over. She had woken up to see Michael on the floor and something large and hairy in the window; what must have been a grizzly bear. It had terrified her like nothing ever had. She felt exhausted again as the adrenalin left her system, and though she had said she wouldn't sleep, truth be told that was all she wanted to do.

A lot of it had to do with knowing Michael would protect her. Though an independent woman, Karen wasn't above admitting that men had their place in life. Michael was a rugged man who was comfortable in the woods, where she was a city girl. She would be fooling herself to think she was his equal in the middle of the forest. And deep down, she knew she actually liked it that way. It wasn't such a bad thing to be beholden to a man, especially if it was one that loved you dearly, as Michael did her.

Of course, all of this she would never admit to him or anyone else for that matter.

What woman would?

Once the fire was going strong, she felt better. Michael made some instant coffee and they sat together on the bed. Michael's eyes never left the broken window, but as the first hour passed uneventfully and became the second and then the third, his guard slowly began to crumble and he began to grow tired.

Karen was sleeping beside him once more, snoring softly, and with the silence of the night weighing heavy on him, Michael felt his eyes becoming heavy, his head dropping to his chest as he drifted off to sleep once more.

Pulled from sleep in an instant, he was so startled he literally fell out of the bed.

It felt like an earthquake was rocking the cabin.

"What's happening?" Karen shrieked from the bed as Michael went to his knees, the drowsiness of sleep washed away immediately to be replaced by adrenalin-fueled alertness. He could feel his heart pounding in his chest like it was about to break out at any second.

"I don't know, stay there!" he yelled and stood up, the entire cabin shaking like a living thing.

The remaining, intact window exploded inward and a large shape appeared before it. Behind it, feeble light seeped in, the new day dawning.

A loud roar made Michael look at the other window, the one shattered hours ago, and he saw another creature there, its long arms reaching in, trying to get at him and Karen. A roar escaped its razor sharp, tooth-filled mouth, one filled with rage and pain.

Pounding came from the front door, the wood rattling in the frame, and Michael knew there was yet another one there.

There were three of the creatures outside the cabin and they wanted to get inside desperately, the claws raking at the walls, their fists pounding again and again.

Snapping out of his terror-filled state, Michael picked up the .38 from the floor where he'd dropped it, and shot one of the creatures. A low howl filled the cabin and the creature fell back, away from the window. He spun and shot the other one at the second window and received a similar howl of pain.

The door stopped shaking and one of the walls of the cabin began to crack apart, a paw twice the size of a human adult hand forcing its way through the hole. Below the clawing hand was the carcass of what Michael believed was a grizzly bear cub. The paw was straining to reach the dead baby and Michael shot the arm, causing the limb to retreat when the bullet hit it dead center near the wrist.

Another section of the wall near the cub carcass began to give and then a different arm came through. Michael could see the fur was darker than the previous one.

He shot at it but missed.

Karen was petrified as she watched Michael shooting the creatures as they came in front of the window, then she saw the cabin wall smashed open and the paws trying to grab at the carcass.

Though terrified, it was easy to see the beasts wanted the carcass badly, and though she didn't know for sure, she gambled she was right as she suggested, "Michael, I think they're trying to get the baby bear! Give it to them!" Karen screamed, realizing what was happening as the creatures attempted to reach the body.

"What? What're you talking about?" he yelled back and shot at a shape in front of one of the windows. He received another howl of pain.

"The baby bear! The bear cub, Michael! They want the body! That's why they're attacking the wall by it. Just give it to them, please! Maybe they'll leave us alone!"

Not having a better idea, Michael did as she said. He ran to the carcass, picked it up and sprinted to the closest window. It was empty at the moment and he tossed the body through the opening, the blanket covering it and all. The blanket caught on the edge of the window frame where glass shards protruded and stayed there, the carcass tumbling out to land messily in the wet earth. It rolled a few feet and came to a stop in a three inch puddle.

Michael took a step back from the window, the gun raised to shoot anything that might appear. Sweat ran down his brow and he was breathing fast. He blinked perspiration from his eyes and waited, his legs weak from the adrenalin pumping through his system.

From his vantage point, he could see the area over the carcass easily, and within a few seconds of the carcass landing on the ground, three creatures surrounded it, the banging stopping.

He watched in amazement as one of the humanoid, hairy beasts leaned over the carcass and inspected it. Seeming almost human, the creature touched and prodded the carcass, as if it was trying to wake the cub, as if it was only sleeping and not dead.

Michael could see that this creature was shaped differently than the others, and he thought he could discern the shape of breasts under the hair on its chest. It was also thinner at the waist and wider at the hips than the other two, which were taller and had more muscle mass.

His guess was it had to be the mother of the baby cub, though now he realized the grizzly bear cub wasn't actually a cub...it was something else, something he never would have believed existed a day ago.

As if in answer to his unspoken question of whether the beast was the mother of the dead baby, the female creature began to wail, a mournful howl that was filled with sorrow and loss. It slowly picked up the carcass and cradled it to its breast, rocking it back and forth as howls of loss rose from its mouth. Michael was taken aback at how human-sounding the wails were. It was chilling.

The two males of the species turned and looked at the cabin, seeing Michael standing there, watching, through the broken window, and they roared like lions, about to begin the attack anew. But the female stopped them with a paw, then gestured to the treeline.

The three began to bark at one another, the sounds resembling a language Michael had never heard before. They went back and forth for over a minute until finally the mother raised its right paw and lowered it, the gesture seeming like a human saying, "Enough, no more debate!"

As one, the three creatures walked into the forest, the female never stopping her mournful wailing, though it did quiet slightly, as if only so much sadness could be had at a single moment in time. Their footfalls were heavy and made loud crashing noises as they entered the forest, as if they didn't care about making noise.

As the seconds passed, the wailing faded and the cabin grew silent, with the exception of Karen's sobbing and Michael's heavy breathing.

"I...I think it's over. Whatever they are, they've left." He turned to Karen. "You were right. They wanted the baby. Like any family would if their child was killed or taken from them."

"Michael, I want to leave this place, right now!" she yelled and began to sob harder.

"We will, let's just give it some time, all right? Make sure they're gone for good." He went and hugged her, the two waiting quietly, praying the ordeal was finally over.

They waited for a full hour, then Michael stood up and said it was time to go. They quickly gathered anything they thought was relevant and then prepared to exit the cabin.

Karen was having second thoughts about leaving, wanting to stay inside where it was safe, but Michael convinced her that the creatures had left for good and they could leave. Walking to the door, he opened it slowly. He looked at the wood on the outside to see large gouges in the facade, looking like someone had used a chisel and a hammer to mark the wood. Long streaks of wood were missing, attesting to the sharpness of the claws on the creatures.

Michael stood perfectly still, his ears straining to pick up the slightest noise other than the birds chirping in the trees, but nothing was amiss, and nothing appeared to attack, so he took a step outside.

The sun was high in the sky, and the ground was slowly drying, but there were still puddles about. Fifteen feet away, his car sat in the sun, looking the same as the previous night. The fenders were covered in mud and Michael saw that the grille was broken from when he'd hit the baby-whatever-it-was. He tried not to look at the bits of blood and fur stuck in the grille.

Placing his left hand on the doorframe, he turned around to face Karen, his back now to the surrounding forest, and he smiled widely. "See, I told you we scared them off. It's perfectly safe."

It was as he was beginning to turn around and walk to the car, that he saw Karen's eyes go wide in terror, her mouth opening to let out a scream.

At the same instant, Michael saw a shadow fall across the threshold, blotting out his own shadow. As he finished turning, he saw a massive paw with long claws coming at his head and then the world was spinning as his decapitated head rolled across the ground to come up near the front tire of the car.

His body stood immobile for a few seconds, not understanding that the head was gone, while blood geysered out of the neck stump to splatter the top of the doorframe. Then the legs simply gave out and the headless corpse slumped to the floor of the cabin, half-in and half-out of the door. Blood spurted out to pool around the body, the sun reflecting in the crimson puddle.

Though his head was severed from his body, for a few brief seconds Michael's brain still functioned, and in those last seconds he saw the same three humanoid creatures charge into the cabin. He heard Karen's terrified shrieks for help, and she called out his name again and again.

Her screams for help went up in pitch as she was eviscerated and dismembered. Watching through the open door, he caught only a glimpse as internal organs, arms and legs were torn off and thrown across the cabin, and out through the doorway, a severed foot landing only a yard from his head.

A single tear ran down the side of his face, then his brain shut down as oblivion claimed him.

In the trees surrounding the cabin, the birds still chirped, the carnage that was playing out in the cabin irrelevant.

Creatures within the forest killed other creatures all the time, it was the way of nature. The strong killed the weak, the cycle of life forever turning.

Minutes later, the three creatures exited the cabin, each covered in blood and viscera. One paused by Michael's headless corpse, tore off the arms, and tossed them away, the action looking as if it was done for sheer spite.

One arm landed on the hood of the car, blood seeping out to trail across the paint to drip into the earth.

In a single line, the three beasts stomped off into the forest again.

They had no choice in their actions this day, for the humans had killed one of their clan, and a baby at that.

The only way the debt could be paid was in blood...and paid in full it was.

PART TWO

CRIME SCENE

Forest Ranger Laura Carson wiped her mouth after vomiting for the second time in as many minutes.

A few of the crime lab techs nearby chuckled slightly but no one outwardly chided her.

It wasn't her fault, and she couldn't imagine how any of the other people around her could look upon the carnage inside that cabin and not feel the same.

She guessed it was because she was still considered a rookie. She had been a Forest Ranger for the Adirondack National Forest in New York for a little more than two months, and most of the other men and women she worked with had been there for years, some as long as twenty.

In that time, her co-workers had witnessed every possible animal attack, hiking accident and sometimes just a natural death, one that went unnoticed for so long that the body would liquefy if it expired inside a vehicle.

It was coming on dusk and the red and blue strobe lights of the State Police squad cars gave everything an ominous glow, creating shadows where normally there would be none.

Gathering herself, Laura walked around the green and white Forest Ranger car she'd used to hide behind, and joined the rest of the ten plus group of civilians, State Police, detectives, and Forest Rangers gathered around the crime scene of the worst animal attack in the history of the state.

"Feeling better?" Mack Richardson, her direct supervisor, asked with a slight smile. He had gray hair and a beer belly, with kind eyes and a thick mustache, also gray. He had taken Laura under his wing when she arrived, as green as they come, but ready to work.

"A little," she replied, but no sooner did she speak then her eyes went to the headless, armless torso in the door to the cabin; she felt her esophagus constricting.

"Don't beat yourself up too badly," Mack said. "I've seen almost everything and this disturbs even me."

A detective walked up and nodded to Mack and Laura. He was handsome with a good build. Laura remembered his name as being Detective John Morrison, because she had talked to him earlier and had noticed he didn't wear a wedding ring.

The second she saw his striking visage, her radar had gone up. Almost thirty, she was beginning to worry that if she didn't find a man soon, she would end up living in her apartment alone with nothing but cats and a goldfish to keep her company.

She had known of a woman like that when she was a child, who lived a few doors down from her house, and she remembered the entire neighborhood called the old woman the 'crazy cat lady.'

She had often thought it would be preferable to eat her gun instead.

"You have anything new for us, Detective?" Mack asked, getting his question in before the detective could speak. "That is, new from what my people already told you."

Morrison shook his head. "Nothing yet, but give the CSI boys some more time."

Mack sighed. "You're people are wasting *mine* and *your* time here, Detective. This was nothing more than a bear attack. A bad one, mind you, the worst I've ever seen, but a bear attack all the same. My people will have to go out and find it and put the bastard down for good before more people get hurt."

Laura knew that when a rogue bear was in the area, it had to be destroyed so other hikers or campers wouldn't be hurt. It was terrible really. This was the bear's natural habitat and it was the humans that were encroaching on its home. But either way, any attacks on humans were dealt with immediately. Deep inside, she took the side of the bear, but her job was to protect the lives of people first, then the wildlife.

One of the CSIs had been standing nearby, listening to the discussion and now stepped up to be seen, clearing his throat politely to be noticed. "It was more than one bear, Ranger," the man said to Mack. "We found at least three different sets of tracks and there's one more thing, something you need to see for yourself." He gestured for the trio to follow him inside the cabin. "It's not pretty in there but then you already knew that." He was looking at Laura when he said this and she knew word had spread about her vomiting bout. Laura saw the name tag sewn into the vest of the man's right pocket—**CSI Edwards**.

Laura was last in line to cross the threshold to the small cabin, her eyes glancing briefly at what looked like claw marks on the door's facade. The instant she entered the structure, her stomach began to roll, but she managed to keep it under control. Mack saw her discomfort and grinned slightly, casting her a brief nod of support.

The interior of the cabin was a charnel house, with the entire contents of a human body spread on every wall, the ceiling and floor. There had been a headless body in the doorway, but after it was processed, it was removed. It was harder to remove what had been a body inside the cabin as it was in more than a hundred pieces.

Blood splatter coated everything but had dried to a dark rust color. Fat blowflies were everywhere, maggots crawling on every surface. It had been more than a week before a ranger had come upon the house and thought to check on it.

That had been a bit of luck as it could easily have been over a month before someone dropped by to inspect the cabin. It was necessary. Sometimes meth labs would sprout up in neglected cabins. In the middle of nowhere and off season, it was the perfect place to cook meth, so the Forest Rangers had to be on guard constantly.

"We know this all belongs to a female," Edwards said as he walked over to the fireplace, where pieces of flesh hung from the mantle like bloody Christmas stockings. "We found her severed head in the corner." He pointed to the bed. "And we found her heart over there." He pointed to the wooden table and chairs. "Her kidney and spleen were found over there."

"We get the point," Mack said, aggravated.

Morrison nodded. "We know the identity of both people thanks to the car out front."

"Who were they?" Mack asked.

"Michael and Karen Benson, ages thirty-eight and thirty-nine. They live—or I should say 'lived'—in New York," Morrison explained. "The cabin was registered to a Marty Benson, a relative no doubt. I had him checked out, but Marty's been dead for two years, a heart attack from what I read."

"Huh, the couple were probably up here to do some camping and then this happens," Mack said. "Terrible. The worst attack I've ever seen and I've seen a lot over the years," he said again. "I tell you, there's something strange about all this, something's not right."

Edwards had been talking to another CSI and now he turned and got everyone's attention. "That isn't the half of it," he said, picking up on Mack's feelings. "Here, come take a look at this." He knelt down and pointed to what looked like a bloody human footprint, only the foot was twice the size of an adult print and seemed to have long claws at the tip of each toe. The claw marks were indented into the wood.

"These are all over the place. One of my guys found three separate prints, each made by what appears to be a different person." He looked at Mack and then Laura. "You got any mutant hillbillies running around in your forest, Rangers?"

"Of course not, this isn't the movies," Mack scoffed. "But then again, who knows what's up in those mountains. We have thousands of acres of land here, and it's patrolled by a total of two dozen Forest Rangers, not much when you think about it. A lot of it is still untouched. Still, I think I'd know if there was some kind of mutant hill folk living somewhere and they sure as hell would have been seen before this."

"Then how do you explain these prints?" Edwards asked.

Mack shrugged. "I can't, but I don't have to. This was a grizzly attack, pure and simple, and as soon as you people are done here me and my people will get together a posse and find the rogue bear or bears and take 'em down."

Mack turned and walked out of the cabin, the discussion over. Laura followed. Once outside, she saw a CSI tech making a mold of one of the large footprints near the edge of the treeline. White plaster was being poured into the print.

Laura had seen enough police procedural TV shows to know that when it hardened, it could be taken out and a perfect mold of the footprint would be available for study.

"Hey, Mack, what do you think about those prints? There has to be a logical explanation," she said.

"Yup, and there is one. Someone found this crime scene before my Ranger did. They thought it would be funny to put on some funny shoes or whatever and stomp around, making a mess and just plain screwing with us. It's someone trying to make us think it was aliens or some such nonsense."

"But Edwards said…" she began but Mack cut her off.

"I don't care what Mr. CSI thinks. I know what's what and this is nothing but a bear attack, a bad one mind you, but that's all. Tomorrow morning, you, me and six other Rangers are gonna go into those woods and find the bears responsible for this shit and put them down before they can hurt anyone else."

"Count me in, too," Detective Morrison said from behind Laura. As he walked up to them, he pulled out a pack of cigarettes and lit it up with the expertise of a long time smoker. He made eye contact with Laura and Mack to see if they wanted one, but both declined with a wave of a hand or a simple shake of the head.

"Thanks for the offer to come, Detective, but I think I'll pass," Mack said. "I don't need no city boy stomping through my forest, and just getting in the way."

"I'll have you know, Ranger, that I grew up on a farm about twenty miles north of Boston," Morrison said. "Livestock, produce, the whole nine yards. I think I can handle myself just fine."

Mack was already shaking his head and his lips were parting to say no, when Laura stepped in. "Ah, come on, Mack, let him come. He might learn a few things from you," she prodded.

Mack closed his mouth slowly, his eyes taking the measure of Morrison, as if for the first time, then he slowly nodded. "All right, fine. If Laura wants you to come, I'll let you. Even if it's just to see you make a damn fool of yourself." He looked at Laura. "But he's your problem."

She glanced at Morrison with a wan smile and then looked Mack square in the eyes, her face serious again. "I think I can keep him in line."

Mack grunted in reply and walked away to talk to two of his Rangers who had come from around the back of the cabin.

"You know, I didn't need your help. I could have gotten my CO to get me on the search party."

She shrugged. "Maybe, but Mack doesn't like being told what to do. If he was forced to take you, trust me, it wouldn't be a pleasant hike. This way is better...for all of us."

"I'll have to take your word for it," he said and turned to face the cabin. "I want to check out a few more things. Care to join me?"

"Sure," she replied and followed Morrison back to the cabin. But he didn't go inside, and instead walked to the right, both of them soon in what could be called the backyard. There was a small section near the treeline cordoned off with chicken wire and overgrown weeds filled the interior of it. Someone had setup a garden at one time in the past.

He walked right up to the back wall of the cabin and began touching deep grooves in the wood; they looked like someone had taken a chisel to the wall. Laura joined him and with the two standing side by side, he said, "These look like more claw marks, similar to the ones on the front door."

She leaned forward and squinted slightly. "I suppose they do; what's your point?"

He traced the marks with the tips of his fingers. "Well, for one thing, there are five marks, like what you'd find on a human hand. That doesn't mesh with Mack's idea that this was a bear attack, does it?"

She shrugged again, something she did often. "It might have been a bear with an extra toe on its paw. It happens sometimes, like with inbred cats. Hell, my mother had a Siamese cat with six toes. When it would get something on the bottom of its paw and then track it around the house, you'd get this weird print thanks to the extra digit. It happens in nature sometimes."

He nodded, as if he was agreeing with her. "Oh, so you're saying we have us a freak bear with an extra toe, is that right? One that decided to go on a killing spree with a couple of its buddies?" He looked on the ground and then took a step back, realizing he was standing in another large humanoid footprint. The print was nearly twice the size of his black leather shoe. "Then how do you explain this?"

"More phony footprints from the hoaxers who messed with the crime scene before we got here," she said. "Look, Detective..." she began.

"Please, call me John when no one's around but us."

She smiled. "Okay....John. I know you seem to want some kind of conspiracy to be found here, but it's all just a bear attack. You'll see tomorrow when we find the rogue's cave." Her two-way radio crackled with static and then Mack's voice came over it, telling her he needed her at the front of the cabin.

"I gotta go, he doesn't like being kept waiting. Give me your card so I can call you tonight and let you know about tomorrow morning."

He reached into his coat pocket and pulled out a business card. With a wide smile, he said, "Sure, here. But tell me the truth, is that why you need it or is it just the excuse you're using to get my phone number?"

She found herself blushing and began to turn away. "I only need it to call you but if you're suggesting that I might need it for something else..." she trailed off. She had butterflies in her stomach now and her knees were weak. She wasn't much of a flirter and she had never been that good with the opposite sex. But there was something about John that put her at ease, more so than any other man she'd known for a long time.

It might have been his calm exterior or the way his gaze never wandered. He always looked her in the eyes, despite her full-fitting shirt that did nothing to hide her 36cs, or her thin waist. She worked out every morning before work, or after if she had a morning shift. She ran five miles every other day and six on Sunday. No man had ever said she wasn't attractive, it was just that all the men in town were a bunch of hicks and she'd never found one she was really attracted to.

"Well, if I'm not being too forward," he said, "then yes, you're more than welcome to use that number for 'something else.' I'm staying at the Red Coach Hotel, room 6. Do you know where it is?"

"Sure, it's the only one in town other than the bed and breakfast on Main Street; it's not hard to find."

"Good, then maybe when you get off duty tonight, you could swing by and we could …uhm…I don't know…talk about the case some more?" He made it sound like a suggestion.

She saw he was blushing slightly, too, and she thought it was endearing. He was as uncomfortable as she was, which meant he wasn't some kind of jerk who hooked up with a woman every chance he got. Her two-way squawked again and Mack began yelling at her to get her ass over to him on the double or she would find herself scooping poop in the camping grounds for the next two weeks.

"Look, I gotta go…" She turned and jogged away.

Morrison watched her leave, admiring the way her butt filled out her work pants. He didn't know what had come over him; he'd never been that forward with a woman before.

One of his faults in his opinion was that he was too shy, and all his buddies had told him repeatedly that if he ever wanted to meet a woman, he had to be more confident. No one could say yes to him if he never had the courage to ask the question in the first place. When he'd met his ex-wife, it had been a lot like meeting Laura, they had just 'clicked.'

Realizing he was all alone behind the cabin, he turned around and gazed into the trees. The forest was dense and he couldn't see for more than a few feet before the foliage blocked anything from view.

He felt a chill come over him and he had the strangest feeling he was being watched. He reached down and touched his pistol where it was strapped under his arm, and was about to take a step towards the treeline to investigate, when Edwards appeared from around the corner of the cabin. "You're wanted out front," the man said and Morrison stopped and turned to face him.

"What's up?"

Edwards gestured with his head to the front. "That old Ranger, the one you were talking to, he has a few questions for you."

Morrison nodded and followed Edwards away from the rear of the cabin, the feeling he had now gone. Later, when he would think about it, he would believe it had all been in his head.

As the two men disappeared around the side of the cabin, the area once more becoming empty, the leaves shifted six feet into the treeline and a large figure began to move away.

It was silent as it walked, its stealth deliberate, the creature only made noise when it wanted to. It had blended into the foliage so perfectly that Morrison could have been standing a foot away from it and quite possibly wouldn't have seen the creature until it was too late.

Within seconds it was gone, the branches it brushed becoming still, as if it had never been there to begin with.

PART THREE

ROMANCE

Detective John Morrison had been in his hotel room for a little over an hour when there was a knock at the door.

Getting up from the chair in the corner of the room, he padded across the floor and opened the door, surprised to see Forest Ranger Laura Carson standing there.

She was wearing a blue sundress with matching sandals and her long brown hair was draped over her shoulders, framing her beautiful face. She was smiling slightly, her cheeks red as she blushed like a school girl.

Morrison blinked in surprise, not expecting anyone to drop by, let alone Laura. He'd thought their playful flirting had been just that, 'flirting.'

"Well, this is a pleasant surprise," he said, the door half open.

"Uh, yes, for me, too," she replied. "Look, if you're busy I can go. I don't want to intrude."

He opened the door as wide as it would go and took a step back. "No, please, come on in, intrude away."

"Thank you," she said and stepped into the room. "I know I should have called first, but to tell you the truth, I didn't think I'd have the courage if I did."

"Then I'm glad you didn't," he said with a smile. "Here, have a seat," he added, gesturing to the chair he'd just vacated. She did so, sitting with her legs side by side, her hands on her lap, crossed one on top of the other, her purse by her left foot. It was the way her mother said proper young ladies should sit and right now she was trying her best to seem like one. After all, she knew how it looked. Here she was, dropping by a man's hotel room without being asked, and a man she just met as well. She knew what her mother would say if she'd been here with her right now.

"Can I offer you something to drink?" he asked. "I have ice, coke and Rum, together or separate." He walked over to a small table near the window, where a bottle of Rum and a six pack of Coca Cola sat. One red and white can was missing from the pack and sat opened but empty.

"Together is fine, thank you." She tried to keep her voice from cracking. God, she was so nervous, too nervous for someone of her age. It wasn't like she was seventeen and her boyfriend was eighteen and they had gotten a room so they could finally have sex. She was an adult, for heaven's sake, a woman of the world.

She let her gaze move about the room, taking it all in. There was a full size bed in the middle with clean sheets and a floral patterned bedspread, the chair she sat on, one window with faded yellow curtains, the table with the beverages, a television on its stand and the door leading to the small, shower only bathroom. The walls were papered with pictures of flowers as well, and though old, were well kept. It wasn't the Ritz, but it wasn't a dive, and for an out of town cop to use as he inspected a local crime scene, it was perfect.

On the end of the bed was a manila folder, a few photos poking out, only a few inches visible. Immediately, she knew they were crime pictures of the bear attack at the cabin.

The crack of a soda can snapped her away from her visual inspection of the room and back to the here and now.

"Ice?" he asked.

"Yes please, and only a little Rum. It's gonna be an early day tomorrow and I want a clear head."

"I hear ya, I usually only have enough to help me sleep. I find it's better than sleeping pills."

She nodded and smiled again as he handed her the plastic cup, one of a set of four, the unused two now sitting alone on the table with plastic wrap covering them. "I would think you have trouble sleeping a lot, what with the things you see," she said, sipping the drink gently, the way her mother would have told her to.

"I'd be lying if I said I didn't." He poured himself a fresh drink and she saw he wasn't shy about the Rum, despite what he'd told her. "I'd like to tell you that I've grown used to it. That I'm hardened to it, but I'd be lying. Other than having a stronger stomach, it still gets me every time I go to a crime scene and see what one human being has done to another. Sometimes I just don't know how it's possible."

"What about the bear attack at the cabin?" she asked and sipped her drink.

"Hmm?" he looked up and she realized though he'd been talking, he wasn't necessarily talking to her; he was just voicing his thoughts.

"The cabin, the two bodies..." she said, trailing off to jog his memory.

"Uh, well, that's different. That was an animal attack. Nature is nature, only the strong survive and all that. It was tragic to see two people killed like that but it's not the same as going into an abandoned building and finding a teenage girl raped and strangled...or worse."

"Yeah, I see what you mean." She wanted to steer the conversation to something a little more positive, but she didn't know what to say.

Then, he did it for her. "So, what made you become a Forest Ranger?"

"Oh, well, uhm, my uncle I suppose. He was one for twenty-three years. He used to let me spend the days with him during the summer. I guess that's when I fell in love with nature. I know that sounds corny."

"Not at all."

"When I was old enough, he got me into the program and here I am."

"Well, you look good in the uniform, anyway," he said with a polite smile that reached his eyes.

"Thank you," she replied bashfully, feeling herself blushing again. She stood up, wanting to take a moment for herself. "May I use the bathroom and freshen up a little?"

"Of course, it's right over there." He gestured to the open bathroom door. She grabbed her purse, and quickly went inside, closing the door softly. She ran the water as she sucked in a deep breath. The Rum in the drink was getting to her some; she wasn't a heavy drinker.

She waited for more than a minute, closing her eyes and breathing in and out, waiting for her heart to slow down. She had never felt this way about a man before and though it excited her, it bothered her, too. She knew nothing about him other than what she felt. He seemed nice enough, but for all she knew, he'd been married three times and divorced just as many, and now had a pile of alimony and a truckload of children to pay for.

When she exited the bathroom, he was sitting in her chair, which meant for her to sit, she had to walk over to the bed, sitting on the end, her purse by her side once more. He was sipping his drink as he watched her, a slight smile creasing his lips.

"So, Ranger Carson."

"Please, call me Laura, I'm off duty," she said quickly.

"Of course," he said coolly. "So, Laura, why exactly did you come here tonight?"

She felt herself blushing again and willed her cheeks to remain cool, though it wasn't helping much.

"I...I don't know really," she replied honestly.

He stood up and walked over to her, sitting down beside her. He was so close she could feel his warmth. She idly wondered if he'd sat in her chair so she would have no choice but to sit on the bed, thus creating the moment she was experiencing.

"I think I do," he said and slowly leaned closer to her, trying to see if his gesture would be reciprocated.

It was and she slowly leaned in to him, their lips moving closer and closer. It was just as they were about to kiss that her cell phone began to buzz, shattering the mood. She slowly pulled back and smiled a little. "I should get that, it might be Mack, my boss."

"Please don't let me stop you, work comes first," he said, and she saw he looked like a little boy who'd been told no pie after dinner. He looked dejected and then some.

She was already pulling the phone out of her purse. She flipped it open, saw the number displayed and said, "Hello, Mom, this isn't really a good time." She was so embarrassed.

Morrison gave her a wide grin and stood up, walking over to the table where he'd left his drink.

"Yes, Mom, I said I'd be there and I will. Look, I really have to go, can I call you later tonight?" She nodded as her mother said something. "Uh-huh, okay, good, yes, fine, okay, I gotta go, I love you, too, okay, bye." She snapped the phone closed and looked at Morrison, who was sitting in the chair again, concentrating on his drink.

"I'm so sorry about that," she said.

"It's fine, really, we all have mothers," he said with deference.

"No, it's just… she's turning fifty-five this weekend and there's going to be a party for her and she wanted to make sure I was going. Of course I'm going, I'm her daughter."

He nodded in agreement.

She sighed, frustrated at the entire situation. But she hadn't come this far to throw in the towel. Placing her phone down, she screwed up every ounce of courage she had and stood up. Fixing her dress with her hands, she walked across the room and stopped in front of Morrison.

"I believe you were about to kiss me?" she said with a smirk, her stomach full of butterflies.

He almost choked on his drink and she chuckled a little, but didn't want to embarrass him. He put down his drink and wiped his mouth with the back of his hand as she slowly leaned over him. Her hands went to the armrests and slowly their lips moved closer. When she kissed him she planned on straddling his legs and from there anything might happen…or so she hoped.

It was just as they were about to kiss that 'his' cell phone began to chirp, and he looked away from her at the last second on instinct, his eyes going to the phone on the table.

"Oh shit, I'm so sorry, I don't believe it," he huffed as he stood up and walked a few feet away, Laura having to back away so he could stand.

"No it's fine, after all, you're on duty here," she said. He couldn't see it, but she was rolling her eyes, feeling humiliated. She had actually gotten the courage to make a pass—or finish the one he began—and once more technology had gotten in the way.

"Morrison," he said into the phone. "Hey, Santoro, yes, I saw the crime scene, yeah, you were right, it was pretty bad. How bad? Okay, remember that guy who was so hopped up on meth that he killed his wife and daughter with a butcher knife, carving them up like they were Thanksgiving turkeys?" He waited for an answer. "Yeah, well, this was worse. Uh-uh, right, I should be back the day after tomorrow. Fine, tell Kowalski he can try it if he wants to, but Martinez is my C.I. and he won't spill if I'm not there; he needs to wait till I get back." He nodded to himself. "Right, I guess we have a special bond, tell Kowalski not to be so fucking impatient, we'll get the dirt bags; they're not going anywhere." He laughed. "And fuck you, too. Look, I gotta go, I'm in the middle of something." More garbled words through the phone. "Okay, I'll talk to you soon, see ya." He hung up and looked at Laura with an apologetic look. "So sorry 'bout that. It was my partner. He would have been here but he had a family emergency."

"No, it's fine, work is work after all."

"Exactly," he replied, as an awkward silence fell between them. Neither wanted to speak first.

A truck drove past the room, causing the walls to vibrate and Laura shifted her feet while Morrison cleared his throat. "Uh, listen," he began, "I haven't eaten yet. Is there anywhere good around here to get a pizza?"

Her eyes lit up with something to talk about. "Oh sure, there's a great little place in the middle of town. You want to go?"

He stood up. "I thought you'd never ask." He grabbed his keys, jacket, gun and holster, cell phone, and glanced once around the room once, making sure he hadn't forgotten anything. Then he gestured to the door. "After you, my lady," he said like an aristocrat.

She curtsied, glad the moment of awkwardness was over. "Why thank you, kind sir," she mimicked and went to the door, opened it, and stepped outside.

He followed, the door closing softly behind him.

Outside, they walked side by side, the moonlight casting the street in a pale glow. It was a small town, but not so small it didn't have restaurants, gas stations and shop fronts.

Despite this, it was only a fifteen minute walk from one end of the commercial area to the other, and the night was cool but pleasant, so Laura convinced Morrison to walk with her, leaving his and her car behind. She did grab her jacket from her car before they left.

It was almost eight and as it was a weekday, the streets were fairly quiet, only a few vehicles on the road and almost no one about as a pedestrian.

Other than an old man walking his dog and an elderly woman hugging her purse tightly to her chest, who was in an obvious rush to get home, they had the street to themselves.

All the shops were closed and Laura told him only the couple of restaurants and the gas station would be open at this time of night.

Morrison chuckled at that. "Wow, in the city, nothing ever closes or if it does it's only from like three a.m. to seven, but it's usually less, like an hour or so.

"The city that never sleeps, right?" she asked.

"That about sums it up," he agreed.

Two teenagers turned a corner from an alley and began walking towards them. Laura spotted them immediately, recognizing them for two boys that lived near her. Out of the corner of her eye, she saw Morrison reach under his jacket and grasp the butt of his sidearm.

Reaching out and touching his arm, she said in a low voice "Relax, John, I know them, they're good boys."

He released his hold on the gun but she could see he was still tense, his eyes never leaving the boys as they approached. When the two teenagers were within a few feet of them, one of the boys said, "Hey, Ranger Carson, how you doin'?"

"Hi, Roger, I'm fine thank you." She gave both boys a wide smile. "Now, you two behave yourself, don't go getting into trouble."

"We won't," they both replied at the same time, then they were past her and Morrison, who began to walk sideways slightly so he could make sure the boys weren't going to double back.

"You can relax, John, this isn't the big city, crime is a rarity around here."

"I know, but old habits die hard," he said. "In the city, if two boys like that are coming at you in the night, chances are you're about to get mugged...or worse."

She chuckled. "Perhaps, but not here." She slid her hand through his arm so they were walking side by side. She liked the feeling of him beside her and wished they were back in the hotel room but knew that moment had passed.

As they rounded the corner and were about to cross the street, Morrison paused, his head held high as he sniffed the air like a bloodhound.

Looking perplexed, Laura asked, "What's wrong?"

"I smell smoke," he stated simply.

"Okay, so what? Someone's got their wood stove or fireplace going."

He shook his head slightly as he sniffed some more. "This isn't that kind of smell. This is the odor of a building burning." He sniffed again, the noise louder this time. "Can't you smell it? It's different than fireplace smoke."

She concentrated on her sense of smell and then yes, she did detect the odor of something burning, more than likely a building or a home. There was something about the odor of a burning house that couldn't be matched by anything a fireplace or wood stove could produce. When the vinyl siding, insulation and wiring of a house began to burn, it left a scent in the air like nothing else. What she didn't hear were sirens. Normally, when you smelled smoke, an accompanying siren of a fire engine would be close by, but the night was silent.

As a Forest Ranger and the town being her home, she knew what she was going to do before she did it. She began walking down the street she believed the smoke was coming from. "Come on, we need to check this out."

He hesitated. "Why? Just call it in and be done with it."

"No, John, it's my duty to investigate. As soon as I know for sure, of course I'll call it in, but not before."

He stomped his foot lightly, aggravated. "But I'm hungry."

She turned to face him, now walking backwards. "We can eat later. Are you coming or not?"

Not wanting to be outdone by her, he began to walk, jogging to catch up. "Of course I'm coming, I'm not gonna let you have all the fun." When he caught up to Laura, he passed her, jogging down the street as if it was a race.

Not wanting to be left behind, she picked up her pace as well.

Following the smell of smoke, Morrison rounded the corner to the second street and then stopped, his eyes taking in the scene before him.

A two-story house was in front of him, and it was burning uncontrollably. Laura came up behind him, her breathing slightly heavy, but nothing compared to his heaves as he sucked in air. She grinned slightly; he didn't jog like she did, evidently.

Laura was already calling in the fire on her cell phone as Morrison began to run across the street and onto the front lawn of the home.

"Wait, where are you going?" she called after him.

"There might be people inside!" was his reply.

As he crossed the lawn, it was clear how terrifying and out of control the blaze truly was. The roof was engulfed in red and orange flames, some shooting twenty feet into the sky. In the midst of the flames, dark, churning smoke billowed in thick clouds, making the home look as if a massive storm cloud was hovering over it.

If only I would be so lucky for it to rain, Morrison thought.

The flickering flames created an eerie glow in the surrounding darkness, reminding him of a large candle caught in a gentle wind. The fire-weakened wood crackled and popped, sending small embers of flaming material into the air. From first glance, they resembled fireflies.

Morrison was so close to the house he could feel the intense heat on his face. He winced slightly, gritting his teeth from the discomfort. He was about to turn away when he heard the distinct sound of a scream come from inside the house.

Someone was definitely in there!

The air was becoming thick with acrid smoke, making each breath he took suffocating and stale. He felt a burning sensation in his nostrils as they started to dry out from the heat. Embers floated down around him like snowflakes, collecting on every flat surface. Some still glowed orange and hot enough to fuse into the fabric of his jacket; he brushed them away before they could do much damage. All around him, the yard was covered in a thin film of ash, looking like tainted snowfall.

Laura came up beside him, grabbing his arm. "What's wrong?"

"There's someone inside the house, I have to go in."

"Are you crazy? It's a fucking inferno in there, it's suicide! Wait for emergency services to get here."

On the edge of her rebuttal, another scream rent the air, one filled with pain and terror. It sounded young, a child's voice.

He shook his head. "By then it'll be too late, I have to go in now." He was already running to the front door as the words left his lips. She called out to him but he couldn't hear her, the blood rushing in his head, pounding like a set of drums. When he reached the closed front door, he raised his right foot and sent his one hundred and eighty pounds of muscle mass behind it. He'd been kicking in doors for over ten years and knew exactly where to place his foot.

The lock gave way easily and the door slammed in, the frame by the doorknob splintered. The second the door was kicked in, air rushed into the house, causing the flames to erupt higher.

Covering his face with his arm, Morrison charged into the inferno, his eyes desperately trying to see through the smoke. He'd learned in boot camp to breathe through his nose, not his mouth, and so far he was able to avoid coughing. One intake of breath through his mouth would be all it would take to start a coughing fit he would likely not recover from. But his nose was a filter, and as he sucked in air, it burned his nostrils but he was able to maintain control. In seconds, thick rivulets of mucus leaked from his nose as the smoke slid into his sinuses.

Another scream came from his left and he saw a set of stairs leading to the second floor. Taking the steps two at a time, he ascended to the landing at the top. The smoke was thicker here and he could barely see. He went to his knees, trying to find air still breathable. Even the nose trick could only go so far and he became lightheaded from lack of breathable oxygen. His eyes teared, rolling through the ash covering his face and he squeezed them shut, ignoring the burning sensation.

The crackling fire was all around him, only the landing devoid of flames, a small pocket of safety.

He saw a hallway leading deeper into the house and doors on both sides. Jumping through a wall of flames, he rolled and came up in a crouch. He coughed a little and thought he would lose it right there, but managed to hold it in. there was a bedroom door on his right, a handwritten sign on it with the word, **TIMMY** in bold red crayon. The sign was burning now, the edges curling, the **Y** in the name already obscured.

Coming to his feet, Morrison kicked the door open, heedless of whether the other side was nothing but flames.

It wasn't.

Inside, a typical boy's bedroom greeted him. On the floor in the corner, a six-year-old boy was covered with a sheet as he hid, crying uncontrollably.

Morrison ran to the boy and scooped him up, the boy crying out and trying to kick and punch.

"Cut it out, I'm here to rescue you!" Morrison yelled as he squeezed the small bundle tighter.

The boy had his own bathroom attached to the bedroom and Morrison ran to it. There was a bathtub and shower there and he jumped into it, turning on the water to full-blast. Standing under the spray, he was soon soaked, as was the boy.

When he was as wet as he thought possible, he ran out of the bathroom, through the bedroom, and back into the hallway.

The hallway had turned into a gauntlet of flames, smoke, and collapsed woodwork. Burning wallpaper whirled through the air like snowflakes in the churning clouds of smoke. The floor and walls were nothing but charred wood, and the moldings on each door were peeling free to twist and bend at odd angles.

The fire was burning out of control and the wall on his right was nothing but a sheet of flame.

He began moving back to the stairs, covering his mouth and nose with the wet sheet protecting the boy. Smoke darkened the staircase, making it difficult for him to see, but he continued forward by memory alone.

He blinked continuously, trying to moisten eyes that were irritated and dry from the cloying smoke. As he reached the landing, he still couldn't see, and his right foot missed the top step, his leg going out into empty air. As he went to put his foot down on what he thought would be the hallway, he found himself falling.

He curled into a ball on instinct, his arms wrapping around the small body in his charge, doing his best to protect him. Morrison gritted his teeth as each step slammed into him, his shoulders and back taking the brunt of most of the fall.

He rolled to a stop at the bottom, coming up against the wall, his legs in the air, his back on the floor. The boy was crying uncontrollably now, his tiny frame shaking violently, while Morrison saw stars from the fall.

Morrison looked down to see his left leg was on fire, the flames three inches long and growing. As if he was swatting at an annoying fly, he calmly reached down and slapped out the flames, then slowly got to his knees.

Thanks to the fall he had stopped breathing through his nose and was coughing uncontrollably. Bits of white light flashed before his vision and he coughed and hacked.

Behind him, the inferno raged on and in the back of his mind he wondered how he had survived it. His wet clothes from a second ago were already drying out from the heat, the moisture sucked from the material. He saw that the rug on the stairs was a carpet of flames, and if he had tried to walk down them, he very well might have never made it. In the end, his fall might have allowed him to escape.

Somewhere inside the house, an explosion sounded, rocking the foundation to its very core, sending burning plaster raining down from the cracked ceiling. The home began to collapse and Morrison began to try and crawl to where he thought the front door was, but as he coughed and hacked, his eyes so filled with burning soot he couldn't see, he began to crawl deeper into the house.

Flames licked at the walls, rolling across the floor like a living thing, and he felt his consciousness fading. The boy in his arms had gone quiet, the body still, but he was too lost in his own suffering to check. Black phlegm came out of his mouth as he coughed, the heat scorching his lungs each time he sucked in air.

His diaphragm contracted and he felt a sharp pain in his chest, idly wondering if he was having a heart attack. That would be the utter irony of his life, he thought. To charge into a burning home and then to die of a heart attack.

He was on the verge of passing out when he felt a strong hand on his shoulder, then another hand grasp him under his right armpit. As he was half-dragged, half-carried the opposite way he was going, he realized he'd been about to crawl deeper into the house and certain death.

"Come on, help me! You're too heavy for me to carry by myself!"

He glanced up through the smoke to see Laura standing over him, her face already covered in soot, her hair hanging over her face, her eyes tearing uncontrollably. She was already suffering a coughing fit and she fought to stay on her feet. The left shoulder of her jacket was burning where debris had landed on it.

Another explosion ripped through the back of the house, shattering every window, glass shards shooting onto the lawn like crystal daggers. If it was physically possible, the inferno actually intensified as more air rushed in to feed it.

Laura renewed her efforts, and with Morrison on his knees, using the last of his willpower and strength, they made their way to the front door.

Only a few feet away, it felt like a mile, but eventually, Morrison felt the outside air hit his face, the cooler temperature reviving him slightly.

With Laura's help he was able to stand up, and with her further assistance, the couple hobbled through the doorway, the small boy still grasped tightly in Morrison's arms.

No sooner did they exit the house then another explosion rocked it, sending flaming pieces of the roof into the air, to spin and wobble before gravity took the debris back down to earth, like small comets shooting through the night sky.

The fire department had finally arrived and was setting up their equipment. Firefighters attached hoses to hydrants and opened the valves, their loud voices calling back and forth to one another. Water rushed through thick hoses, resembling giant gray pythons, the men dowsing the burning house with water, trying to prevent the flames from spreading to nearby homes.

Three firemen in bright yellow jackets and pants ran up to Laura and Morrison, helping to get them further away from the burning house. Another man took the boy out of Morrison's arms and the exhausted detective let him, too tired to argue. The man ran to a pair of waiting paramedics, who put the boy on the grass and began to check him over.

Laura and Morrison were helped to the back of a fire truck where they sat on the bumper. When handed an oxygen mask, Morrison took it greedily, sucking in great lungfuls of clean air. His coughing had subsided but his lungs were burning in his chest like he'd swallowed a gallon of molten lava. Beside him, Laura was also breathing with an oxygen mask, though she looked in better shape than him, as she had only been in the burning home for a few seconds and hadn't breathed in as much smoke.

Still, she was thankful for the oxygen.

"Some first date," she said, her voice muffled from the mask.

Morrison pulled the mask from his face and replied, "You think this one was good, wait till the second one." He was smiling as he said it but then his visage grew serious. "But really, thanks for coming in for me. If you hadn't, I don't think things would have ended so happily."

She only nodded in reply and patted his arm, then both of them concentrated on breathing with the masks.

A few minutes later, Morrison saw the boy he'd saved on a gurney and being rolled into the back of an ambulance. Taking off the mask, he crossed the road and joined the paramedics that were closing the rear doors as they got ready to leave.

"How is he?" Morrison asked one of the paramedics, a short man with a belly and a receding hairline.

"Smoke inhalation and a few bruises, but he'll be okay." the short paramedic said.

"Too bad about the rest of his family, though," the other paramedic said and pointed to the front lawn of the house.

Morrison followed the man's gaze to see three firemen hovering over two prone bodies, a man and a woman. Both were badly burned to the point of being unrecognizable and were definitely dead. Morrison assumed it was the boy's parents, and only hoped they'd died of asphyxiation from the smoke before the fire had gotten them. As he watched, a fireman covered the bodies with blankets, covering the heads as well.

"Look out, it's comin' down!" a fireman yelled as he charged out the front door, his voice barely heard through his mask.

Morrison looked up at the house to see it was collapsing in on itself, the fire finally weakening the main supports to the point they could no longer sustain the second floor.

The once perfect house was nothing but a funeral pyre now, the flames totally in control, consuming the structure inch by inch. A breeze swept across the flames, whipping a blast of superheated air across the front lawn, where it wilted flowers and leaves on the bushes curled in on themselves. Pieces of heat-warped siding peeled off the house, falling in fiery embers to the ground, while bricks tumbled from the chimney, and shriveled shingles and melted tar from the roof dripped like molasses, to steam and hiss in the dirt.

Clouds of steam from evaporating water from the fire hoses battled for dominance with the smoke, as the walls of the home fell in one at a time.

Finally, a crackling sound floated on the wind as the house gave up the last of its supports and the entire structure crumbled into blazing debris.

His face and clothes covered in black soot, Morrison looked on, not wanting to think that only a few minutes ago, he was inside that inferno.

He felt a coughing fit coming on. He pulled the mask off, leaned over, and hacked up a dark wad of black phlegm. As he spit, it dribbled down his chin and onto his shoes. Wiping his mouth clean, he felt a little better, his airway finally clear. He figured a few more of those and he would be back to his old self.

As the ambulance with the little boy drove away, two more arrived. As the passenger and driver of the closest ambulance hopped out of the cab, one went right for Morrison while the other went to Laura.

Both were led to the rear of an ambulance where they climbed inside, the doors slamming closed. One paramedic stayed with them, checking to make sure their oxygen was okay while the other went behind the steering wheel. Moments later, they were rolling through the crowd of onlookers and then onto a clear road. The siren wasn't on, there was no need.

"I don't need to go to the hospital, I'm fine," Morrison told the paramedic sitting across from him.

"Its protocol, sir, they'll check you out and if you're fine you'll be released tonight. Both of you," he finished as he glanced at Laura and smiled. She returned his with one of her own. She reached out and touched Morrison's arm. "Be patient. John, we'll be done before you know it."

"Yeah, I guess so," he sighed. With nothing to do, he fixed the mask on his face, then stretched out on the gurney he was sitting on. Laura was across from him and she gave him a smile too, trying to stay positive, her eyes twinkling in the soft glow from the single bulb in the ceiling of the vehicle. She realized since she'd met Morrison, she was smiling a lot more...and she liked it.

He stretched his left hand out to her and she took it, the two of them holding hands, like a couple of teenagers at the movies for the first time.

After Laura and Morrison were checked out at the hospital, they were released with a clean bill of health.

Other than a few aches and pains, Morrison was fine, the smoke he'd inhaled not life threatening, though it would take a few days for his lungs to clear. Laura was in even better shape, showing no signs of being in distress as she had only been in the house for such a short time.

They took a cab back to the hotel, as that was where Laura's car was and she needed it to get home as well as report for work in the morning. It was going to be a long day, hiking through the woods. Grizzly bear dens weren't out in the open for all to see, and she knew it would take one of their expert trackers to find it, and even then it might remain hidden. Odds were the posse would travel for miles before finding the den.

Despite the busy night, they never managed to get that pizza, and instead had dined on sandwiches from a vending machine in the hospital waiting room, as the cafeteria had been closed.

Unlocking his hotel door, Morrison stumbled into the room, Laura right behind him. Though she was tired from everything, she didn't really want to leave yet and she fell into one of the chairs while Morrison went and fixed himself a drink.

As he put the liquor bottle down and drank the Rum neat, he offered her some but she shook her head, saying, "Isn't this where we started?"

"Yeah," he chuckled slightly. "I suppose it is, though this time I hurt a lot more."

She stood up and walked over to him. "Oh, poor baby, you did take quite a beating."

He didn't reply, there was no need. His clothes were covered in soot, and both of them smelled like two burnt logs leftover in a fireplace. He had a few scorch marks on his jacket and was glad it was flame retardant, as most clothes were nowadays.

Laura's cell phone rang and she answered it, speaking softly for a few moments. When she hung up, Morrison was looking at her expectantly. He could tell the call was business.

"That was one of my friends at the hospital, she's a nurse," she explained. "The boy you saved is doing fine."

"Yeah, but I expect that he's an orphan now," Morrison said sadly. "I wish I could have saved his folks."

"Hey, that's not your fault," she admonished him. "You did what you could and it's a miracle you were able to save that boy. Besides, he has an aunt flying in tomorrow from Connecticut. So he has family. This is a terrible tragedy but he'll survive it, he's not alone in the world."

"That's good," Morrison said, slightly dejected. "Still, this was a night that kid will never forget. He'll wake up screaming for years, I guarantee it." He finished off his drink and walked to the bathroom. "Look, I'm gonna take a shower. Will you wait for me when I'm done?"

"I uhm, I think I might lea..."

He cut her off. "It's fine, really, you don't have to make any excuses. Look, if you're here that's great, if not, I guess I'll see you in the morning." Before she could reply, he turned and went into the bathroom, closing the door but not all the way in. It was still open a quarter of an inch.

She stood in the room, hearing the water begin to run in the shower, then a few low groans of pain as Morrison began to undress.

Should she leave? True, they may have had a moment earlier, but it seemed fate kept getting in the way, but now, hours later, did she still feel the same way about him? Did she want to become entangled in a relationship? Or worse, did she really want to be that woman who has one night stands with men she'd only met that day?

But Morrison wasn't like most men. The way he'd charged into that burning house, as if he had no fear, knowing people needed saving. That was something she had rarely seen outside of Hollywood action movies. He had saved that boy, almost losing his life in the process, and now another human being would continue living because of him.

He was polite, smart, handsome and well fit, all the qualities she looked for in a man but so far had not found them...at least not all in the same guy.

Biting her lip, she tried to decide if she should leave or wait.

Morrison let out a deep sigh as the hot water cascaded over him, sluicing down his back, the tiny pinpricks massaging his aching body.

He closed his eyes, letting the tension he'd been feeling wash away. Thinking back to the burning house, he now had to accept how truly terrified he'd been. Burning to death was one of the worst ways to die, and if Laura hadn't come into the house to search for him when she did, more than likely he'd be dead now, as well as the boy.

When he thought of the boy he smiled, feeling a sense of pride he hadn't felt in a long time. Sometimes, going from crime to scene to crime scene, seeing the worst of humanity, it was good to see a bright spot in the life of the child.

Sure, the boy had lost his parents, but he still had family that would take care of him. He would be fine...in time.

Glancing down at the bottom of the shower, he saw gray swirls circling the drain from his soot-covered hair. Even though he'd cleaned up a little at the hospital, he found that the soot had gotten into every crevice of his skin.

He heard something on the other side of the shower curtain and looked up, his ear cocked to the side to keep it free of the water spray so he could hear better.

"Laura, is that you?" he called, not understanding what she would be doing in the bathroom. If she had to use the toilet, surely she would wait for him to finish showering.

Reaching slowly for the curtain with his left hand, he unconsciously curled his right into a fist behind his back, just in case it wasn't Laura, then parted the curtain.

"Hi, I thought you could use some company," a naked Laura said as she entered the shower, the water immediately plastering her hair to her head.

He looked down at her from his extra six inches of height and frowned slightly, aware of his nakedness, but not letting it show in his manner. He also did his best to keep his eyes from popping wide open like a wolf in a cartoon as he stared at Laura's shapely body.

Her breasts were all but perfect, each one defying gravity. The nipples were erect and he could see small goosebumps surrounding them from when she had exposed them to the air after disrobing. Her abdomen was flat and tight, her belly button cute. His eyes went lower, to the junction of her thighs, where her manicured pubic hair was. She was neatly trimmed, but not shaved, and he liked that. He didn't understand what the fetish for entirely shaved women was nowadays. To him, they all looked like eleven-year old girls instead of full grown women. Then again, maybe that was the idea.

Her thighs were strong and muscular, curved in all the right places, a small birthmark on her left inner thigh. As he took in her beauty, he believed she was the most beautiful 'real' woman he'd ever seen. The only jewelry she wore was hanging around her neck on a silver chain was a stone pendant, green, about the size of a silver dollar. It seemed to glow in the light of the bathroom. He hadn't seen it before because she'd kept it hidden under her dress.

"Are you sure you know what you're doing? It's been a long day...for both of us. I don't want you regretting anything in the morning." As he said this, he prayed she wouldn't change her mind now. In his head, he was already imagining how he would make love to her, how he wanted to posses her.

She reached up and wrapped her arms around his neck, her nipples brushing the hair on his chest, causing them to stand up even more in arousal, their faces now only inches apart. "John I've never been so sure of anything in my life. You could have died tonight, and so could I if I'd gone into that house with you at the beginning when you first entered it."

Her gaze was penetrating and he nodded, understanding her completely. What they'd shared this night was something few people ever did. They had been wrapped in life and death and had come out on the other side whole.

Maybe tomorrow would be different, but as he held her in his arms, the warm spray of water splashing onto their heads, for at least this night, they were soul mates.

He leaned over so their mouths made contact, their tongues exploring one another. His hands began to slide across her back, exploring every curve, the arch just above her ass. As their kisses became more passionate, he reached down and cupped her buttocks—one in each hand—and pulled her close, his now rock hard member trapped between them. As he began to gently slide himself up and down between their slick flesh, she slowly began to moan louder.

He gently grabbed her by her hair and spun her around so she had to lean over and place her hands and forearms on the shower wall. He reached up and redirected the shower spray so it wasn't in the way, then slid his right hand between her legs, caressing the smooth lips within. She moaned louder, arching her back when he slid two fingers inside her, then out, then back again, a smooth motion that had her bucking her hips in pleasure. While his right hand was busy, he used his left hand to cup her left breast, massaging the erect nipple between his fingers. She began to breathe harder as he then slid three fingers into her. She gasped, and her legs began to tremble and he knew he'd brought her to an orgasm. But he wasn't done yet, not even close.

Though divorced, the one thing his ex-wife never could complain about, even when signing the papers, was that he was a bad lover. Truth was, the reason for the divorce was his job, as it was with most cops. He was too dedicated to the police force and she had always come in second...or that's the way she'd seen it. He hadn't argued, knowing deep down she was probably right. He had been emotionally distant and there were nights he hadn't wanted to talk at all. How could he tell her about the latest murder he'd had to investigate or the last mugging that had gone wrong or a home brutal invasion?

He bent Laura over a little more and then bent his legs so he could lower himself so he was directly even with her ass. After positioning himself just right, he gently slid his rock hard member into her.

He absently thought he was being reckless at not using a condom, but the little voice of caution was pushed down deep. He was too overcome with passion to stop now even if he wanted to, and if there were consequences of this night, he would deal with them later, though he highly believed that if Laura had a sexual disease she would have said something.

He slowly began to pump, and each time he withdrew, hesitating for a brief second, he would then slide back in. It was so warm and inviting and he opened his mouth and let out a low moan of his own in pleasure. She was tight, but not too tight, and with each pump of his hips, they grew more in synch with one another.

As he began to pump harder, she began to pant, a low moan escaping her lips each time he was totally inside her.

He felt himself grow lightheaded from the pleasure, and he pulled out, not ready to cum yet but knowing it had been a while, but he didn't want to look like a teenager experiencing his first time.

When he was completely out and stayed out for a few seconds, she sensed he wanted to do something different, and surprised him by turning around, cracking a smile, then going to her knees before him.

Opening her mouth wide, she engulfed him whole, the tip of his member touching the back of her throat. With her right hand on the shower wall for support, she grasped her left hand around the base of his shaft and slowly slid it up and down in tandem with her mouth.

The feeling was indescribable and he let out a low moan, which elicited a chuckle from her as he sucked and slurped.

She began to move her head faster, then she slowly twisted her hand and the combination soon had him exploding and grunting in ecstasy. She removed her mouth and he sprayed her neck and breasts with his seed, the water washing it away almost immediately.

She stood up, going on her tip toes and they kissed passionately once more. He pulled away and gently nibbled her right earlobe "We're not done yet," he whispered into her ear, "but let's dry off and continue this in bed."

She smiled in reply and stepped out of the shower, grabbing a towel and padding out of the bathroom on tiptoes, while he dried off quickly in the bathroom.

There was a small bottle of mouthwash left for guests and he took a second to swig a capful. Spitting it into the sink, he walked into the room to see Laura was under the covers already, her towel lying on the floor.

The bedspread was on the floor at the foot of the bed and she was sitting under the covers so that the sheet and blanket were at her belly, her upper body exposed for him to see, her nipples still erect, letting him know how aroused she was.

"That's an interesting pendant you're wearing," he said. "I noticed it in the shower but was a little busy to comment on it."

She reached down and picked it up from between her breasts, twisting it back and forth in her hand. "My uncle gave it to me," she said as she thought back to years ago. "He said he found it one day when he was out searching for some lost hikers that had gone way too deep into the mountains. He said he was ten miles easy from the closest cabin, way up in the mountains. He didn't think anyone had been there in hundreds of years, he was so far in. He found it by accident, kicked over a rock and there it was. He had it made into a necklace. I haven't taken it off since he gave it to me."

"Interesting story." He tossed his towel away, not caring where it landed, then hopped into bed with the energy of a ten-year-old boy scared of monsters under the bed. She laughed at his playfulness and soon they were wrapped in each other's arms.

After a minute of kissing, he pushed her down and said, "Now it's your turn." He slowly began to kiss her breasts, focusing on each nipple, then he let his tongue glide down her stomach. He tickled her belly button with the tip of his tongue and she elicited a playful giggle. "Stop that, it tickles."

He said nothing, but went lower, his lips brushing her pubic hair. Then he was at the juncture of her thighs and his tongue licked out, catching her clitoris the way he used to do to his ex-wife. Evidently it worked on all women because a minute later, Laura was shaking and arching her back as she orgasmed yet again.

As she came, she reached down and grabbed his head by his ears and pushed his head into her, his nose and mouth becoming squished as her thighs squeezed his head tightly. As she moaned in pleasure, he found he couldn't breathe and after a second, he had to push with his arms to free his head.

As she lay looking up at the ceiling, a sheen of perspiration covering her flawless skin, he sucked in a breath of air. Wiping his wet mouth on the sheet, he crawled up to her and began to kiss her neck, right where it met her shoulder. He trailed the tip of his tongue up to her right ear and began to nibble on her earlobe.

As she lay still breathing hard, he slid on top of her. His member was right between her legs, the tip of his cock touching her inner lips. He was ready to go again.

"This time we take it slow," he whispered into her ear between kisses.

"Well, John, not too slow, fast is good, too," she purred and pushed him over, then climbed on top of him and quickly slid onto his hard member.

As she began to ride him like he was a bucking bull, he pulled her close and kissed her once more, his arms wrapped around her waist, his eyes closed as he relished the pleasure he was giving and receiving.

When he was able to pull back from her lips to take a breath of air, he had to agree with her and said, "Maybe you're right, fast isn't half bad."

Then she kissed him again and he was lost in the moment, the rest of the world forgotten as two human beings became one.

PART FOUR

HUNTING PARTY

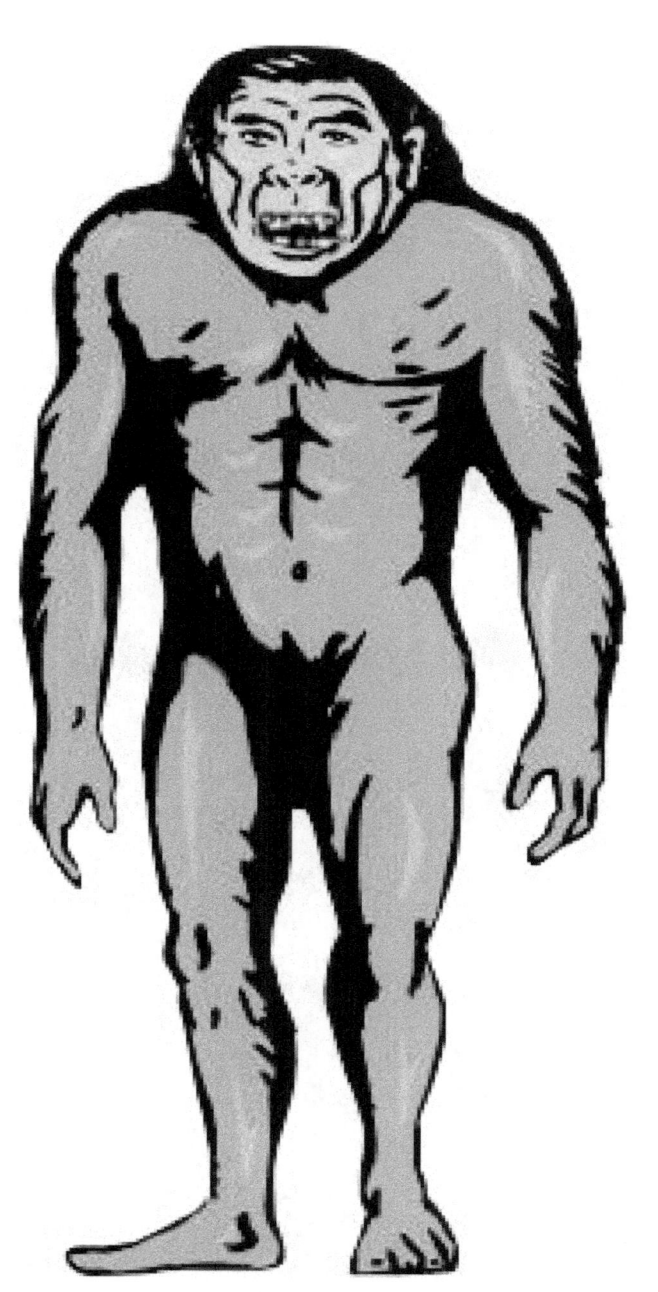

The next morning, Laura and Morrison woke early and made love again, then Laura's cell phone rang. It was Mack, informing her of where to be for the search party for the rogue grizzly bear.

She was to be there by seven a.m. and was instructed to fill Morrison in. Laura didn't bother to tell Mack that John was right next to her; her personal life was her own, after all.

Morrison dressed quickly and Laura drove them both to her house, where she went inside and changed into her Forest Ranger uniform. Morrison stood by her car and smoked a cigarette. She was in and out in less than ten minutes and he was very impressed by this. Most women would have taken three times as long, but Laura was more practical than most. As she ran down the steps with her gun and holster in hand, she slowed when she saw he was grinning widely.

"What's wrong? Why are you looking at me like that?" she asked, suspicion creeping into her manner.

He shook his head slowly, "No reason, just thinking."

"About what?"

"About what a great time I had last night...and this morning."

She climbed into the car and he did the same, flicking his spent cigarette into the street.

"Me too, but if you don't mind, when we get back to the cabin, I'd prefer it if we keep what happened to ourselves."

"Oh sure, I understand completely," he said. She was about to say thanks when he said, "You're embarrassed to be with me."

She opened her mouth to rebut his statement, shocked he would even think such a thing, when she turned to face him and saw he was smiling even wider.

"Very funny, as if I'm not self-conscious enough right now," she said.

"Sorry, I couldn't help myself." He leaned over and kissed her cheek, nuzzling her neck with his nose. "I better get this in now so I don't get caught later."

She turned her head fast so that their lips were only an inch apart. Then she grabbed him by the back of the neck and kissed him passionately. When she released him, Morrison was breathing heavily.

"Wow, what was that for?" he asked.

"Like you said, we better get it in now." She turned the key, started the engine, and pulled into the street. "That will have to do until tonight, when we get back to your hotel room."

Beside her, Morrison was still sucking in air, her passionate kiss taking him completely off guard.

* * *

They arrived at the cabin where the bear attack had happened an hour later. Laura saw that it looked as if she and Morrison were the last ones to arrive.

There were four other Forest Ranger vehicles parked along the driveway and she parked behind the closest one.

Morrison and Laura got out of the car and walked the short distance to where a small group of men—all in Ranger uniforms with canteens and backpacks—stood in a circle around Mack, who was talking. When Mack saw Laura and Morrison, he stopped and turned to face them, speaking to them directly.

"Well, well, look who decided to show up. It's so nice of you to grace us with your presence, Ranger Carson."

Mack looked annoyed and she wondered why. Though gruff, he was usually nice to her and had once said he thought of her as the daughter he'd never had.

"Sorry, Mack," was all she thought to say.

Mack gave Morrison a dirty look, then another to Laura as he glanced over their shoulder at the one car. She realized Mack had seen her pull up with Morrison in the same car and figured he must have an idea why. But he said nothing more and Laura wasn't about to give him information that was none of his concern. What she did on her own time, and who she chose to spend it with, was her business.

Mack looked away from her and back to the group of men.

"As I was saying, we had a tracker coming in this morning to help up us but he couldn't make it, cancelled at the last second. But we'll be fine. Bill Morton here is a damn good tracker in his own right."

A Forest Ranger in his late forties turned to look at the other men. He wore a baseball cap with the National Forest Service logo on it. He was strong and fit, with a thick brown beard with streaks of gray running through it. He looked like the classic mountain man.

"I know these mountains like the back of my hand," Bill said. "If there's a rogue grizzly out there, I'll lead you to 'em."

"Good, that's what I want to hear," Mack said as he looked at the rest of the men. "Okay, so before we go, let's make sure we're ready for anything." He faced each man one at a time and said, "Okay, Carl, you have the first aid gear, right?"

Carl Menotti, a thirty-year-old Ranger with dark skin and a clean-shaven face, nodded. His family was from Sicily and he was an immigrant. He had come to America when he was fourteen, flying over in a plane, though he was always teased that he had taken a boat like in the old days.

"Got it right here, Mack," Carl said, his accent still noticeable despite living most of his life in the states. "I made sure to pack extra doses of snake anti-venom, too."

Mack nodded. "That was a good idea, Carl, you can never be too careful." He turned to face the next Ranger, a young man in his mid-twenties with blonde hair and piercing blue eyes. He looked like he would be more at home on a beach in sunny California than in the mountains of New York State. "Josh, did you bring the Sat phone like I told you?" he asked.

"Yes, sir," Josh Brady said. He held up the Sat phone.

"Good. Remember, I'm only letting you on this team 'cause your father made me. One wrong move and he'll have my ass, so no screw-ups. You do what I tell you to do, when I tell you to. Got it?"

"Yes, sir," Josh replied.

"Must be nice to have the mayor as your father, hey Joshy boy?" Bill joked, but there was a hardness to his voice. "Means you don't have to work to get ahead like the rest of us."

"Shut it, Bill," Mack snapped, then turned to face the next man in line.

"You bring the extra artillery like we talked about, Wayne?"

Ranger Wayne Kowalski, a man in his late thirties, with dark brown hair, nodded. When Laura looked at him, she saw he was covered from head to toe in ammunition belts. At his feet, an open duffel bag was filled with shotguns mostly, as well as a few deer rifles.

"Sure did, Mack. I got it all right here," Wayne said.

"Good," Mack agreed and addressed them as a group once more. "As soon as I'm done, everyone needs to take a weapon and then we'll head out with Bill in the lead." He turned to face the last man, who was standing to his right. This man was at least thirty pounds overweight with three chins, and looked as if he'd get tired walking across the office to get coffee, let alone going on a long hike through the mountains. He looked to be in his fifties. He hadn't been always fat, but a thyroid imbalance a few years ago had added greatly to his weight.

"Are you sure you want to go with us, Mike? You can still bow out. No one will say anything; you've done your time. I know I said I wanted at least six or seven rangers, but we can do it without you."

Mike Fogarty shook his head, his chins shaking back and forth. "I'm good, Mack, I can do this," he said, his voice low and rumbling. He was a heavy smoker, too, and Laura sometimes wondered how the man was still upright.

"I'm a Ranger and damn it I'll do my part. If you guys are goin' into those mountains, I want to be there with you watching your backs," Mike said.

The other men liked what they heard and began patting Mike on the back, telling him they were proud to have him on the team. Mike was a popular man, he always had a kind word to say or a joke to lift the morale if it was low.

Laura liked him, too, she just didn't think he was fit enough to go into the mountains with the rest of them.

"All right then, we're all set. Get a weapon and get yourselves together; we leave in ten minutes."

As the men moved to get a gun from Wayne, Laura took the opening when she saw Mack was alone, and walked up to him. "Mack, can I have a word?"

He turned to face her. "Sure, but it better not be about your boyfriend over there," he said snidely and looked at Morrison, who was busy watching the other men.

She chose to ignore his quip, instead saying, "It's about Mike. Look, Mack, I know you and everyone else like him a lot, but are you sure he can handle a long hike in the mountains? We may have to go miles in before the day is over, climbing around or through God knows what. I don't think he's up to..."

He cut her off. "Now listen, Laura, you know I'm fond of you but I hardly think you're in a position to tell me who I can and can't take with me on a search party. Mike is a good man, and if he wants to come, I won't stop him." He gestured to Morrison as the detective walked up; he was finishing the process of lighting a cigarette. Mack reached out and plucked the cigarette from Morrison's lips. He dropped it on the ground and stepped on it, twisting the sole of his boot to make sure the butt was out.

"And no smoking, damn it. For one thing, if you smell like an ashtray, every animal in a mile radius will know you're there. And two, that's how we get forest fires, from damn city boys who flick their butts when they're done with them, not caring where they land, to then smolder." He glanced at Laura one more time. "Get a gun from Wayne, Laura. We're leaving in five." He walked away to talk to the other men.

"Cheerful fellow," Morrison said as he stared down at his destroyed cigarette. He really wanted to smoke that, too.

"He's a good man, John, just not the smoothest. I guess when you've done the time he has in this forest, you're allowed a little leniency in etiquette," she said.

"Hey city boy, you want a gun?" Wayne called out to Morrison.

"No, I'm good with this," Morrison said and patted his Glock 17 in its holster under his arm. "Besides, I think I'll let you mighty hunters bag the bear when we find it."

"Suit yourself," Wayne said with a shrug of his shoulders.

Bill had wandered away from the group and was searching the treeline in the same place the footprint mold had been made. Laura saw him enter the trees, and a few seconds later reappear with a wide smile on his face.

"I picked up the trail," Bill called out to the others. "Something big definitely went this way, maybe more than one."

Mack rallied the men. "Okay, Bill's got something so let's get movin'. Single file with Wayne taking last position. Any questions?"

"Yeah, I got one," Carl said. "Who gets to keep the pelt when we bag the grizzly? I bet it'll make a nice rug."

He received a bout of laughter and chuckles from the rest of the men, and Mack couldn't help but grin himself. All the men were pumped for the hunt. Bagging a grizzly bear was always something to brag about at the bar in town over a few beers.

"I'll tell you boys what I'll do. The man who fires the killing shot gets to keep the hide. Deal?"

"Deal," Carl said and the others joined in.

The men began to enter the forest, one at a time. Laura and Morrison were in the middle. The order went Bill, Mack, Carl, her and Morrison, Josh, Mike and Wayne.

There was no clear path, Bill leading them past deadfalls, through thick foliage and over half-buried boulders. The men talked in low voices, chatting about everything from the latest baseball game and who would be traded next season, to Wayne's new pickup truck with four wheel drive and an extra wide rear bed.

Laura and Morrison talked a little, but mostly kept quiet. However, they did steal glances at one another and slight smirks were passed between them. Morrison kept thinking about the previous night and how passionate Laura had been. Now, seeing her walking in front of him in her Ranger uniform, even though he'd experienced it for himself, it was hard to believe she was the same woman. A few of the other men joked with Morrison, teasing him about being a city boy. Morrison was wearing casual shoes while everyone else was wearing hiking boots. Laura had told him the shoes would be fine if that was all he had and she'd been right; he wasn't having any problem walking. He suspected the men just wanted another thing to tease him about. He was craving a cigarette but knew he wouldn't be smoking until this little adventure was over. Just feeling the pack of cigarettes in his pocket was driving him crazy.

An hour into the hike, Bill finally raised his right hand for everyone to stop while he checked for a sign of the bear they were hunting. Up till now, Bill had been able to catch minute signs that something had been through in the past week, but it was becoming harder and harder to follow the trail, as if whatever had made it was becoming more aware and was growing more careful.

They moved out after a minute and the hike continued.

A half hour later, surrounded on all sides by dense foliage and trees, Bill spotted something that had him saying, "No one fucking move."

"Why not?" Morrison asked, but before he could move, Bill turned and pointed at him with an accusing finger. "I said don't move, damn it!"

"What you got, Bill?" Mack asked while sipping from his canteen. He was tired but still felt strong, knowing he could go for hours if necessary.

Bill shook his head. "Nothing good, I can tell you that."

"What the hell do you mean by that?" Carl asked from nearby. He, Mike and Wayne were sitting on a boulder, resting. Mike was breathing heavily, his face covered in sweat. He looked exhausted. Laura wondered if the man was going to have an attack right now on the trail. She swore to herself if he did, she'd resign before she carried the fat bastard back to the cabin.

Bill pointed to five rusted cans hanging together from a nearby tree, barely visible in the leaves. Laura saw a trip wire was attached to the cans. She followed it to the tree, then down the trunk, and eventually saw where the wire was a few inches off the ground, only two feet from where Bill was standing.

"We stumbled on an old trap leftover from the pot growers."

"Pot growers?" Morrison said. "The pot farms were shut down years ago by the Feds."

Mack shifted position but didn't move. "Sure did, but those bastards had traps all through these mountains to deter anyone from gettin' too close. The farmers may be gone, but the traps are still out here. Every now and then a hiker stumbles upon something, gets hurt, and we have to send in a helicopter to get them out."

Bill studied the makeshift alarm for a few more seconds before pulling a hunting knife from a sheath on his hip. Kneeling down, he cut the wire. Immediately, the cans rattled to the ground, the sound muffled by the leaves coating the earth.

"We must be close to one of the old fields," Bill said. "Best to tread lightly."

"Okay, time to move out," Mack said. "Everyone follow Bill exactly, don't meander off his course. Try and step in the footprints of the man in front of you. You need to think of this forest as a giant minefield."

Bill began walking again, Mack following right behind him. With a heave of his bulk, Mike stood up, wiped his forehead with his arm, and began walking.

Josh and Wayne helped Mike over a fallen tree and then everyone was off again, single file through the forest.

Morrison glanced over his shoulder at Mike, then leaned in close to Laura so only she could hear him. "That guy doesn't look too good."

Laura snuck a look at Mike and nodded her head in agreement. "I know. He never should have come. Damn men and their macho posturing. I swear, John, ever since I joined the Ranger Service I've had to prove myself twice as hard 'cause I'm a woman, but just because Mike has a set of balls between his legs he gets treated better than me."

Morrison couldn't stop the grin creasing his lips. "Well, let me just say that I'm glad you don't have a set of balls between your legs. If you did, last night in the shower might have been awkward."

She punched his arm playfully and they both laughed.

"You two got something to share with the rest of us?" Mack asked, like the chaperone on a field trip; he began to walk backwards.

"We're fine, Mack, just talking about yesterday at the cabin," she said.

"Uh-huh, well quit conversatin' and pay attention where you're walking. You're uncle may have known these woods like the back of his hand, but we both know you have a lot to learn." His face softened. "And I don't want anything happening to you."

Laura saw the man she knew so well shine through, the man who had taken her under his wing and taught her the ways of being a Forest Ranger. "I hear you, Mack. And thanks."

He gave her a curt nod with his chin in reply. His face once more grew serious and he cast Morrison a hard look that said 'city boys aren't welcome in my forest.' He turned around and began walking correctly.

Josh picked up his pace so he was even with Laura for a few seconds. "He means well, Laura, you know that, right?" He brushed his blonde hair out of his eyes.

"Sure, I do," she replied. There had been a time she thought she and Josh might have been an item, but after talking to him over drinks one night she discovered he was as shallow as they came. Nice, but shallow.

Josh dropped back into line again.

Overhead, birds squawked to one another as they circled the area. It was a beautiful day, despite the reason they were out in the forest.

A distant snarl from an animal cried out to their right and Laura saw Morrison reach for his gun, nervousness clearly written on his face.

"Relax, John," she told him. "It's just a Fisher-cat."

"Is that anything like a cougar?" he asked in a low voice, his eyes scanning the surrounding trees for signs of movement. The ground was covered in a thick layer of brown pine needles.

She laughed. "No, it's like a big weasel. Trust me, you're safe."

She saw his face soften and he let go of his gun. Now he felt silly. "Thanks for the info, I feel a lot better now."

She didn't know if he was joking or being serious, and was about to ask him, when from behind, Carl suddenly screamed in pain, the echo reverberating through the trees, floating over the entire mountain. Birds in the overhead tree canopy took flight, disturbed by the disruption to their once quiet habitat.

Everyone turned around at the same time to see what was going on, weapons up and ready. Carl was a few feet off the path Bill had made and his right foot was now caught in a rusty bear trap.

"Damn it, what the hell did I say about following Bill?" Mack growled as he ran to Carl, the other men right behind him.

"Jesus Christ it fucking hurts!" Carl yelled.

"Quiet down, you damn fool," Mack hissed. "Between your yammering and yelling, anything in the area will know we're out here."

"Like I give a fuck!" Carl snapped. "Mack, I have a goddamn bear trap on my leg!"

Stating the obvious, Mike said, "Oh man, that looks like it hurts."

Carl stopped huffing and puffing and his face froze in amazement. "You can't be that fucking stupid, Mike. Of course it fucking hurts!"

Mack leaned down and inspected the leg after cutting the material of the pant leg away. The teeth of the trap had bitten in right over the ankle. Blood seeped from around the teeth, but not too badly.

A bear trap was designed to trap the prey, not necessarily kill it. He turned to Bill and waved him closer. "Bill, give me a hand with this, will ya?" Mack said as he prepared to grab the trap with both hands and pry it apart.

Bill got down next to him as the others all surrounded them, watching intently. Mack stopped working and looked up at the faces hovering over him, blocking the sunlight. "Will you people back the hell up already? Give us some room to breathe!"

A few mumbled apologies floated through the group and the men took a step back.

"Damn it, Carl." Mack hissed. "What did I tell you about following behind everyone?"

"I'm sorry, Mack," Carl said through shallow breaths to deal with the pain. "I had to take a piss. I thought I'd stop for a few seconds and then be right behind everyone again. Shit, you think I wanted this?" he scoffed.

Laura stood beside Morrison. She could see the look of empathy in his eyes for Carl. "Carl will be all right, John," she said. "Once we get him back, he can get a tetanus shot and get bandaged up. Just cross your fingers his ankle isn't broken. It can happen when the trap snaps shut."

"You know that I can hear you, Laura, right?" Carl hissed through gritted teeth.

"Oh...sorry, Carl," she said.

"Okay, you ready, Bill?" Mack asked as he readied to force open the trap.

"Go for it," Bill told him.

Mack began to grunt as he separated the teeth. Carl let out another yell of pain as the bloody steel teeth were slowly removed from his flesh. Blood began to seep from the wounds the instant they came out.

"Okay, Bill, get his leg out," Mack said through gritted teeth. The spring might have been old and rusty but it was still as strong as the day the trap had been set.

Bill yanked Carl's foot out of the trap and Mack let the sides go. The trap clanged shut again, the snitch sound filling the air and making everyone cringe.

Mack stood up as Carl leaned over to touch his leg, fingertips gingerly exploring the wound.

"Wayne, grab Carl's first aid kit and patch him up, okay?" Mack said as he turned to Bill and added. "Why don't you go scout ahead a little and check for more traps." He slapped Josh on the shoulder. "Why don't you go with him, too." Josh nodded, then he and Bill moved away, beating the surrounding brush with the tips of their rifles.

"Okay, as for the rest of you, we might as well take a break while Carl gets fixed up. Then we'll see what we're gonna do next."

PART FIVE

ON THE TRAIL

Once Carl's leg was bandaged, the search party was on the move again. Carl was lucky in that his ankle was only sprained, and though Mack told him to go back, he refused. With Wayne to lean on, Carl trudged on, wanting to see the hunt to the end. He joked he wanted the grizzly hide for himself.

Bill led the team uphill, deeper into the mountains. Sometimes it took him as long as ten minutes to find the trail he was following, and most trackers would have lost the scent hours ago. But Bill was good at his job and he continually found something to keep the hunt going. Sometimes it was a broken twig or an overturned rock, and every once in a while he found an actual footprint.

The first time he found one, he called Mack over to him and pointed out the print.

"What do you make of that? Don't look like any grizzly bear print I've ever seen," Bill mused.

Mack had rubbed his chin with his hand as he studied the print. It was twice the size of a human being's foot and looked a hell of a lot like the ones found back at the cabin.

"I don't make anything of it," Mack said. "I have no idea what this means," he whispered. "But I want to keep this between us, don't tell the others."

"Why not?" Bill asked.

"Because I don't want to spook them or start a debate."

"About what?"

"About what the hell kind of creature made this footprint."

"So, what then? You don't think we're hunting a rogue grizzly anymore?"

Mack shook his head. "Honestly? I don't know what we're hunting, but I know it killed two people and it's in my forest, so either way it needs to be killed before more people run afoul of it. You agree?"

Bill nodded. "Sure, I'm with you one hundred percent. Okay, we'll keep it quiet."

"Good," Mack turned to join the others who were resting ten feet away.

"For now," Bill said under his breath.

Two hours later, the sun high in the sky, they took a break to have lunch. It was well past noon and they had been hiking for over six hours with only the occasional ten minute rest. The team was deep into the mountains, miles and miles from any official paths designated for hiking.

No hikers with a lick of intelligence would be where they were, because if they got hurt or lost, no one would ever find them.

Which made it a perfect place for a grizzly bear to make its den.

Laura and Morrison sat a few feet away from the others, talking and chatting as they ate sandwiches Mack had seen to bringing. He had simply stopped at the local diner the night before and put in an order for cold cut sandwiches he would pick up the next morning. He put it on the town's bill.

"It's so beautiful up here, isn't it?" Laura asked as she ate.

Morrison nodded. "I guess so, though I would have preferred not to have walked all morning to get here."

"But this is where pure nature is, not sullied by man," she said. She pointed to a bird's nest high in a nearby tree. "You see that nest?"

He nodded.

"That nest belongs to the Red-bellied falcon. It only makes its nest at five thousand feet and only in one area of the forest. And they mate for life."

Morrison's left eyebrow went up slightly. "Oh really? And are we still talking about the falcons or are you hinting at something else?"

"I'm talking about the birds, silly. If you mean us, we're people; we have minds of our own to decide what we want and don't want. It's not the same thing."

"Uh-huh, if you say so," he said and took a bite from his sandwich.

"I did," she replied back, wanting to get in the last word, a little upset at what he was inferring. She wasn't some needy woman that had sex one night with a man and wanted to marry him the next day.

"Okay then," he said, wanting to get the last word on her.

They turned on the fallen log they were sitting on to face each other and made eye contact, then burst out laughing together, realizing how foolish they were being.

When the laughter abated, Morrison leaned forward and whispered, "Look, I had a great time last night and if you want, I hope we can repeat it again and again. But we just met, let's take it slow."

"I agree," she smiled. "Slow it is."

"But not too slow," he joked, reminding her of last night.

They laughed again, at ease once more with one another.

"Okay people, let's get moving, we have to be close," Mack said. He stood up and clapped his hands to get everyone's attention.

"Well, our den leader says it's time to get going," Laura said. She policed her food wrappers and water bottle, Morrison doing the same. All the men did this, knowing the only way to take care of Mother Nature was to leave a place exactly the way they found it. 'Take pictures and leave only footprints' was a motto the Rangers lived by.

Laura glanced at Mike to see how he was doing, the large man already standing. Though he looked tired and was breathing hard, he was doing well, and once more Laura was impressed. She never would have believed the man would have made it as far as he had.

It took a few minutes for everyone to gather their gear, and with Bill once more leading the way, they headed off.

Twenty minutes later Bill stopped cold, raising his hand to stop the others. Laura wondered if he'd found another pot grower's trap.

Mack snuck up next to him and leaned in close. "What do you see?" he whispered.

Bill pointed to an area of dense trees about twenty feet away and to the right.

"I saw something move over there, something big." Bill raised his rifle, sighting down the barrel as he searched the forest.

Mack almost jumped out of his skin when Bill yelled, "There!" and began firing.

The second he began firing, the others followed his lead, all sending bullet after bullet into the area Bill had indicated. Bark from trees flew off in large splinters as the barrage of lead tore up the woods.

Leaves were shredded from branches as the entire area was bombarded by deer shot and bullets.

The only two people in the team that weren't shooting were Morrison and Laura, who saw nothing to shoot at and retained control. Morrison didn't shoot for the simple reason that if he couldn't see his target, he wouldn't fire blindly. It was a habit he practiced as a cop in the city. Shoot wildly in the city and who knows where the bullets could end up. Laura didn't shoot because she followed Morrison's lead, though her sidearm was drawn and ready. Though Mack had told her to get a rifle before they began the hunt, she had passed, knowing the others had more than enough firepower without her carrying a rifle, too.

After a full minute of non-stop shooting, Mack began to yell for everyone to cease fire. It took him yelling for almost another minute before the team finally stopped.

"Christ almighty, when I say to cease fire, I mean to cease fucking firing!" Mack yelled as he glared at the men. He turn to Bill and snapped, "What the hell did you see out there, Bill! So help me if it was a fucking deer, I'll have you doing camper inspections for the rest of the year!"

"It wasn't a deer, Mack," Bill rebutted. "I swear. It was big, as big as a grizzly...bigger even."

"All right then, let's go see what you guys shot...if there's anything left of it after that shit you all just pulled." He turned to face everyone. "No one better fire again without my say so, you hear me?"

Each man either nodded or told him yes, most looking like scolded children. Morrison smirked slightly as he watched the scene unfold. And they thought he was the buffoon of a city boy, he mused. All of them needed to have a good look in the mirror.

Mack led the team this time with Bill right behind him. There was no need for Bill to lead now. The section of trees that had been shot up was as plain as day. Branches were snapped off, some hanging by thin bits of bark. Tree trunks looked like Swiss cheese. Fresh leaves covered the ground, the lower braches now denuded and bare.

"Okay, everyone spread out and see what you can find," Mack ordered when the team was only a few feet from the beginning of the destruction of nature.

They split off in pairs of two, Laura and Morrison sticking together and going right, Mack and Bill going left, Carl limping with Wayne, the two men going straight, and Josh and Mike hung back, searching the section of where the first trees showed signs of bullet holes.

"Christ, how could anything have survived that onslaught?" Morrison asked Laura as they kicked leaves aside, looking for something. No one found a carcass of any kind, so whatever Bill had seen had somehow escaped alive.

"I don't know, maybe Bill didn't really see anything. It might have been a shadow, a trick of the light or..." Laura trailed off as she stopped walking and knelt down. She had spotted a wan reflection of light on the ground. "Hey, I found something."

Morrison joined her. As he bent over next to her, he touched the dark crimson droplets with an index finger, then rubbed the liquid together between his fingers. When he sniffed it, the aroma of copper came to him "It's blood all right. Looks like they actually hit something."

Laura stood up and called out, "Mack, over here, we found blood!"

Everyone stopped what they were doing and practically ran to her position, wanting to see what she'd found. When Mack and Bill joined them, he bent over and did the same as Morrison had done.

"Yup, it's blood all right."

"No shit," Morrison whispered to Laura, who smirked.

Bill stepped out of the circle the men were in and began to study the ground around them. It took him all of thirty seconds to pick up the trail again. "Got more drops over here. It leads higher into the mountain." He checked the prints and saw another large one, human in shape, only bigger. He waved Mack over to him so he could speak to him privately. "Mack, it looks like we got more of those crazy footprints, too. What do you want to do?"

"What do I want to do?" Mack asked. "I want to find out what the hell we just shot and finish it for good."

"Maybe we should go back and get more men, fuck, call in the Army. Whatever this thing is, it's gotta be big," Bill reasoned.

"To hell with that," Mack scoffed. "We just proved it ain't bullet proof. And there's eight of us and only one of it." He frowned, looking disappointed. "Don't tell me you're scared, Bill."

Standing taller, Bill's jaw grew taut. "Me? Hell no, I'm not afraid of anything. You want to go and get this thing, fine, let's get it done."

Mack nodded, proud of his friend. "Okay then, lead on and we'll follow like before." He turned to the rest of the team. "Okay, Bill found blood and it leads into the mountain. We're gonna follow to where it leads and finish this shit once and for all. You men with me?"

A raucous cheer went up and no one seemed to care about the noise they were making. Then again, after all the gunshots, the men cheering was like a small branch dropping to the earth right after a giant tree was knocked down by lightning—it was inconsequential.

The hunting party began to set off, Bill with his face pointed down at the ground as he followed the trail. Laura and Morrison were still standing together when the last of the men passed them.

"I like how Bill took credit for the blood you found," Morrison said.

Laura shrugged. "It doesn't matter, I don't care."

"So, what do you think?" Morrison asked.

"About what? We might as well see this through, one way or another."

"I agree," he said. "Just think; all this for one grizzly bear."

As they began to walk, she said, "Well, either way, it'll soon be over. The bear is bleeding, it won't take too long to track and kill it."

The trail was easy to follow; any of them could have done it. Laura could see the bear they'd shot was bleeding badly, worse than when they'd first discovered the blood. It was probably from moving as it walked. As the bear kept walking or running, the wound opened more.

Leaves were splattered with blood, branches broken, rocks disturbed, kicked over as if by dragging paws.

ANTHONY GIANGREGORIO

"The animal is getting clumsy now," Bill said as he inspected a deep groove of disturbed soil in front of him. "It's wounded, disoriented from blood loss. It must be hurt bad. It wouldn't surprise me if we come over a hill and find it dead before us."

"Great," Carl said disgusted. "We come all this way and I didn't even get to shoot the damn thing out in the open. And if it's dead when we find it, how do we know who gets the hide?"

Mack glanced at Carl, looking aggravated. "Who cares about that, Carl. Just shut up and keep your eyes open, and that goes for the rest of you, too."

"How 'bout we take a break?" Mike asked from the back of the line. He was breathing harder than before. Mack and Bill were setting a faster pace now that the prey was so near.

"No, no breaks now. Sorry, Mike but you're just gonna have to tough it out. I'm tellin' you guys we're close."

The trees around them were growing closer together, some so close that the men had to turn to the side and slide through. Mike had the hardest time and there was at least one time when Laura thought the man would have to be grabbed by the arm and yanked through. It reminded her of Winnie the Pooh when he got caught in the hollow tree trunk.

The trail of blood led them past the thick trees and up to what resembled a wall of rock thirty feet high, but was in fact a giant boulder. There were enough cracks and crevasses for the team to slowly make their way to the top.

118

Mike almost didn't make it. He was halfway up when he felt himself slipping, his bulk simply too much for his arms to hold up, when Wayne and Josh reached him and saved him from a bad fall.

With his hurt ankle, Carl had a tough time of it, too, but Wayne helped him past the rough spots. When he reached the top, Carl breathed a sigh of relief. "Man, I don't want to think about when we have to climb back down again."

"One thing at a time, Carl," Wayne said as he wiped his hands on his pants.

"We should have brought climbing gear," Bill said to Mack as the two men scaled the boulder.

"Now how the hell would I have known that we'd be climbing mountains?" Mack snapped. "All we have is the one rope in case someone fell into a ravine or whatever. We can use that to make the climb back down easier."

Morrison helped Laura the entire way and a few times she did the same to him. Her legs were strong from running and she fared well. Morrison was huffing and puffing by the time he reached the top and she had to help him over the edge.

"Man, I've got to quit smoking," he gasped between sucking in air.

She helped him to stand. "Look at it this way; it'll be easier going back down."

"I guess," he said and looked around himself, the rest of the team close by. They were standing before a large, open glade surrounded on all sides by huge pine trees, at least a hundred years old. Knee high grass waved gently in the light breeze.

Off to the left of the glade, was a drop off that went down to a steep ravine filled with jagged rocks. If someone fell down there, they'd be dead instantly with no chance of survival, if not from the fall then the rocks would impale them.

At the opposite end of the glade a large valley could be seen, one that would be almost impossible to see from the air, thanks to the thick canopy of trees.

A stream meandered through it, the water's edge lined with clay.

Once Bill was rested and ready to move out, he began to search for signs of the prey's blood, and after a few minutes, he found it again. There was a large spot of blood in the general shape of a human hand, only larger, right at the edge of the rock wall, where there was a small opening perfect for someone to grab onto. It was apparent the prey had used the handhold to scale the wall.

Mack joined Bill who pointed out the bloody print.

"That doesn't look like anything a bear ever made, Mack. I think we should tell the others what we've found."

"No, damn it, don't say anything. All it'll do is have everyone asking a lot of questions there are no answers for. Just wait, when we find it, we'll have our answers. It's probably got some kind of abnormality, a birth defect maybe." Mack turned away from Bill and called everyone to him, then they walked out onto the glade,

Bill following the blood trail once more. Against the green grass, the red blood stood out easily.

When they reached the middle of the glade, the trail stopped, the blood gone, but there was a large spot where it looked like something big had fallen, trampling the grass beneath it. Bill knelt down to examine the crushed grass and found even more large footprints.

When the team had first reached the glade, birds could be heard singing to one another in the nearby treetops, but suddenly, it became deathly quiet. Even the wind stopped blowing, the grass still. It was as if the woods had grown silent, as if it was waiting for something to happen.

Laura and John held hands, foreboding filling them but not understanding why. It was something deep inside them, a base instinct from back when men lived in caves and dinosaurs roamed the earth.

"Something's wrong, the birds have stopped singing for some reason," Bill said as he looked left and right, around the glade, searching for signs of danger.

All eight of them stood in a small circle in the very center of the glade, each with their heads moving back and forth. It was a sunny day with light cloud cover and it was at this exact time that a thick cloud chose to block out the sun, thus casting the glade in shadows for a few seconds.

As if the instant the sunlight was blocked for a few precious seconds was a signal, the trees around the glade suddenly exploded with more than a dozen hairy figures, some as tall as eight feet, the shortest towering over six feet easily. They were covered in tan and brown hair from head to toe, more than half carrying clubs made from thick tree branches.

They snarled and shrieked what sounded like war cries as they charged at the humans, who stood absolutely still, frozen in shock.

"What the fuck are those things!" Wayne yelled, snapping the rest of the team back to reality.

Mack put two and two together and yelled, "That's what attacked the cabin! That's what we've been hunting!"

"What about the fucking grizzly bears! We were supposed to be hunting bears!" Carl yelled as he stared in utter horror. The creatures were twenty feet away and closing fast, there was no time left to do anything but fight.

Mack said as much a second later. "It's too late to run! They waited for us to get out here and now there's no place to go! We have to fight! Shoot the fuckers! Shoot them!"

Then there was no time for talking, the creatures among the Rangers.

Carl was the first casualty. With his bad foot, he wasn't able to dodge a blow of a club when one of the creatures came at him. Carl barely had enough time to elicit fear before the club was coming down on his head. Like a watermelon hit by a sledgehammer, Carl's skull imploded, brains and bone matter spraying in all directions.

Standing behind Carl, Mike stood with his mouth wide open, astonished at the sight of Carl's head becoming nothing but red pulp and sagging skin.

Carl's body remained standing as the club came down and his head exploded, but a second later his knees began to shake, the arms twitching spastically. Then the headless body simply slumped to the ground while blood spurted from the neck hole to bathe the grass scarlet, the warm liquid reflecting the sunlight as the plasma pool grew in size.

Wayne began to fire his shotgun the instant Mack gave the order. As one of the creatures came at him, he leveled his weapon and fired. The blast took off the beast's arm at the elbow, leaving a mess of jagged bone and spurting blood. The beast barely slowed down, though it seemed puzzled by its missing arm. It howled in anger, and came at Wayne again.

Wayne racked another shell into the chamber and fired again. As the beast came at him, a fist-sized hole appeared in the hairy abdomen, the internal organs sliding out to splash in the grass. The creature took a few halting steps forward, and Wayne felt fear touch his heart at the sight. If the creatures wouldn't go down when gut shot and a limb blown off, what chance did any of them have?

But the beast steps faltered and it tumbled face first into the grass. Wayne whooped in victory, lined up another creature in his gun sight, and fired. This one he got in the head as it charged a frightened Josh.

As the beast ran at Josh with arms wide, razor sharp claws glinting in the sunlight, its head suddenly disappeared in a glorious spray of blood and brain matter. Josh turned to see the headless thing coming at him and he screamed long and loud, more scared now than when the creature still had a head. Bright arterial blood geysered out of the neck stump to rain down on the grass. As the beast fell over, Josh waved to Wayne in thanks.

Wayne was about to return the wave when another creature came up behind Josh and stuck its claws into his back, then raised its arm. Josh found himself a foot off the ground, and when he looked down, he saw four bloody claws jutting out of his chest. Oddly, he didn't feel any pain.

The creature raised him high and then used its other clawed hand to grasp Josh firmly, and with a mighty heave, the creature spread its arms apart. The claws sliced through Josh's ribcage and flesh like he was made of nothing but paper, and as Wayne watched in horror, Josh was bifurcated, his intestines splashing onto the grass as his mouth opened wide for a silent scream.

With organs sliding out of Josh's exposed torso, his feet twitching beside him, the creature tossed the two parts of Josh in opposite directions. Wayne saw the body parts fall away to be lost in the tall grass.

Meanwhile, Mack was shooting as fast as he could squeeze the trigger, Bill right by his side.

Using deer rifles, their shots seemed to have almost no effect on the creatures. Mack saw that only Wayne's shotgun was doing any real damage. Mack shot a beast in the stomach and watched it bend over from the impact, but a second later it was up and charging again.

Mack and Bill dodged away from a creature with a club and then came up firing. Together they blasted the beast with lead and finally the thing went down, its dark brown hair now coated in hot sticky blood.

Mack heard someone scream from his left and turned to see Mike trying to run away from one of the beasts. But the creature was quick and agile, where Mike was like a bloated whale on land. Mike made it all of six feet before the beast landed on him, taking him down hard. Mack thought it looked a lot like one of those nature shows where the lion pounced on the weakest zebra. As Mike was taken down, his shotgun went flying and landed in the grass near Mack.

Mack was on a slight rise of land so he was able to see Mike as he fell into the grass. He wished he hadn't. As Mike fell face first, he tried to roll over so he could protect himself, but the beast was on him too fast for Mike to do anything but scream for help.

The claws of the creature were out, and it slashed at Mike again and again, cutting his face to ribbons and opening his chest wide. As the claws sliced into Mike's belly, thick folds of fat, yellowish in color, resembling sour cottage cheese slid out. Mike shrieked in agony as he was torn apart, gutted. Mack saw bits of Mike go flying. First an arm was torn off, then a leg, then internal organs. Intestines were pulled out like rope, the creature fascinated by how much it could yank out of the large man. By now, Mike was mercifully dead, his body still, the blood only seeping into the grass instead of pouring out. Bored with the dead man, the beast tossed the body part in its hands away from it and turned to find more prey.

Wayne had blasted another creature, taking off more than half its neck and a section of its face. But still the beast came on. As it lunged for him, Wayne rolled to the side, coming up firing. The monster was right in front of him, a perfect shot that would most definitely kill it.

Wayne squeezed the trigger.

Only he didn't get the satisfying jerk of the shotgun, followed by a nice hole in the creature, instead all he got was a dry *click*.

"Oh shit," he whispered, realizing he was out of shells and there was no time to reload.

The creature raised its arms high in the air, its shadow falling over Wayne, then it came forward, claws flashing in the sun, Wayne yelling for help, until his screams turned into wet gurgles.

Mack saw Wayne go down and heard the man's cries for help. The creature was hunched over the body and Mack couldn't see what it was doing, but a second later, the beast stood tall, holding Wayne's severed head in its hand. It leaned back and howled, then snuffed something that sounded a lot like laughter. With a heave, it tossed the head deep into the glade.

Bill and Mack stood side by side, and to Mack's left fifteen feet away, he could see Morrison and Laura doing the same.

That was all he saw of the couple; he had enough to deal with all on his own.

Mack and Bill had been working as a team, one firing while the other reloaded, but they were slowly being surrounded by the creatures, another three going after Morrison and Laura. Mack was shocked to see that after all the lead that had been flying; only four of the monsters had been killed.

"This doesn't look good, Mack," Bill said as he reloaded, Mack holding off the beasts for the moment. It seemed they had learned what bullets could do and weren't just coming at the two men haphazardly anymore.

"No shit," Mack replied.

Bill reached into his pocket and pulled out a hand grenade. "I got this. I can throw it at 'em or if we have no choice we can get them in close and use it."

Mack's eyes went wide when he saw the hand grenade. "What the hell are you doing with that on a bear hunt?"

Bill shrugged. "Don't know, figured it was better to have it and not need it than to need it and..."

"Yeah, Bill, I know the damn saying. Hold off on it, they're too damn fast if you try and throw it at them, and it won't do much good unless you get lucky. As for the other thing, well, we're not there yet."

Bill put it back in his pocket and began to fire. "Okay, reload, Mack, I'm good."

Mack did as he was told, Bill now holding the creatures off. The creatures never stood still for more than a second, running back and forth in front of the two men.

Mack's eyes caught the glint of the sun on metal in the grass nearby and he saw it was Mike's shotgun. If they were going to win this day and live to tell about it, he knew he needed to get that weapon.

"Cover me!" Mack yelled to Bill and he ran for the shotgun.

"Wait, where the fuck are you going?" Bill screamed. "Don't leave me alone!"

Mack heard Bill calling to him in the back of his mind, his focus now on getting the shotgun. As he ran, his heart pounded in his ears.

One of the creatures saw him running and turned to go after him. With the beast only a few feet away, Mack fell to his knees and scooped up the shotgun.

As the creature loomed over him like something out of a horror movie, Mack squeezed the trigger, praying a shell was ready to go and in the chamber.

The report seemed loud to Mack, louder than it should have, and he wondered if it was because of the adrenalin flooding his system. They said in a crisis, you could have heightened senses.

The blast struck the beast in the left leg, sheering it off at the knee.

The beast tumbled to the ground, off balance, blood shooting from the stump. Mack was on his knees right in its trajectory, and as it fell on him, he screamed for help, squeezing the trigger on the shotgun again and again. The booms were muffled each time, but by the last one, the back of the beast blew out and the shotgun barrel poked through, the muzzle covered in gore.

Almost by sheer willpower and determination alone, Mack started to crawl out from under the carcass of the beast; it felt as if he'd been crashed by a fallen tree.

He finally managed to get free, and as he came to his feet, triumphant that he'd taken one of the beasts down, he never saw the one that came up behind him.

He spun, already about to fire, but the creature used its club to knock the shotgun aside. The weapon went flying, the barrel bent from the impact.

Mack gazed up at the creature as it glared down at him. He saw the sharp teeth, the quivering lips, the pug nose, the glittering eyes that seemed all too human. Trying to make sense of what he was seeing, he realized the creature looked a lot like a gorilla and a human melded together.

He was so mesmerized by the beast up close, that he never felt any pain, never had time to scream, or feel fear as the creature brought the club around in a wide swing that connected with Mack's head like a baseball bat to a ball.

Mack's head was knocked from his shoulders, the skin ripping and tearing like tissue paper from the force of the blow. It rolled into the grass where it promptly disappeared.

Mack's body was already falling to the side from the blow, blood spurting out of the neck stump, his hands flapping back and forth, his legs kicking as if he was having a seizure. In seconds this all stopped and the body was still.

"No! Jesus Christ, no! Mack!" Bill screamed when he saw his friend go down. Bill began firing at the beast that had killed Mack, as it roared and dodged out of the way of the bullets hitting it.

As Bill began firing on the beast that had taken down Mack, wanting revenge for his friend, the other creatures were able to make their move, coming up on Bill from behind. Bill, at the last moment, sensing he was being surrounded, jumped to the side as a clawed hand swiped at him, the massive hand barely connecting. The claws had been so close that one talon knocked Bill's hat off, leaving behind a deep scratch in his scalp.

Blood began to seep from the non-fatal wound, rolling down the side of his face and into his shirt collar. Bill fired his rifle again and again, but knew it was hopeless. When the rifle clicked dry, he knew it was over.

He was going to try and run but one of the beasts cut him off and he stopped running and turned to face the beasts as they slowed and glared at him, knowing they had caught their prey. They snarled and huffed, flexing their clawed hands in anticipation of ripping him apart.

"Come on you fuckers, take me, I'm ready," Bill said in a low voice. As he spoke, he reached a hand into his jacket and pulled out the hand grenade.

As the creatures let out a loud roar of victory and charged Bill, he pulled the pin on the grenade. His eyes were closed and his lips were moving; he was saying a silent prayer for his soul to find heaven in the afterlife.

Only one creature was able to inflict pain on Bill, making a large gash on his shoulder, before the grenade went off, killing Bill and three of the beasts. Human and animal body parts went flying in all directions, as well as rocks and dirt.

A hairy arm landed twenty feet away, while a head plopped down thirty feet away, more than half the hair on the head burned off.

As the dust settled and the smoke began to clear, a small hole was left in the soft earth.

Morrison and Laura had been shooting at anything that moved, but so far their handguns had done no serious damage to the creatures.

Off to the side, near the drop-off to the ravine, they stood back to back and fought for their lives.

"What the hell are these things?" Morrison yelled as he shot at one of them. The creatures were fast and it was hard to hit what he shot at.

"How the hell should I know?" Laura yelled back as she fired at a dark brown beast. She was in shock from seeing everyone being killed and mauled and at the sight of these monsters from her imagination. She was counting her shots, making sure she saved one for herself. If it looked like she was going to be trapped, she planned on eating a bullet first.

"You're a Forest Ranger, aren't you? These things live in the forest!" Morrison screamed back.

"I've never seen or heard of these things before. They look like those pictures of Bigfoot I saw as a kid, but that's impossible, they aren't real!"

Morrison shot at one and didn't know if he hit it. "Well, they sure as shit look real to me!"

An explosion went off twenty feet away and a cloud of dust filled the glade. Laura had seen Bill and Mack over that way and now, as the dust cloud drifted away, she saw there was nothing left, no human bodies, not even the creatures.

Her eyes scanned the glade quickly and she realized only she and Morrison remained of the search team. At the same moment she came to this realization, the creatures seemed to figure it out as well.

There were four left in total, the other beasts either dead or wounded to the point they couldn't fight. Together, the creatures turned and began to charge Morrison and Laura.

"Oh shit, they're coming for us!" John yelled. "Come on, we can't fight them!" he pulled Laura after him as he ran for the drop-off.

"No, we can't go that way!" she yelled, trying to stop him from dragging her. Her weight was still enough to stop him and he was pulled up short, almost falling to the ground.

"Well, we can't stay here!" he snapped back.

Like a heard of buffalo were charging, the heavy footfalls of the creatures thundered closer.

Laura turned around just as the first beast reached them. The creature had a club and swung it at Laura, the club low to the ground. Laura barely had time to register what was happening before the club hit her on her left side of her chest and sent her flying into the air.

As she went flying, she caught a brief glimpse of Morrison as he was attacked by another creature. The detective fired three times into the beast's chest before the creature was on him. But it didn't lash out, instead only wanting the man with the gun to stop shooting it. When the creature reached Morrison, it shoved the man away. The differentia in the weights of human and animal was more than double and Morrison found himself thrown backward, his feet leaving the ground.

"Nooo!" he yelled as he was lifted into the air. He reached out for anything to grab onto as he flew closer to the drop-off.

"John!" Laura screamed, seeing him about to go over the side, knowing he was dead. For one brief second, their eyes made contact, then he was over the edge and gone, his cry fading as he fell. It didn't echo long, seeming to cut out after only second.

Laura landed on the ground, and rolled through the grass to end up on her back. She stared up at the sun, bits of darkness clouding her vision as she struggled to stay conscious. The sun grew blurry as tears welled up in her eyes, and she tried to suck in air. She felt pain in her side and knew ribs were cracked or broken from where she'd been hit.

Though too stunned to move, and knowing death was only a moment away, she could do nothing but lay there and wait for the creatures to arrive.

The sound of heavy footfalls came to her and she struggled to rise, wanting to escape. She wanted her gun so she could kill herself, but it was gone, knocked from her hand when she was tossed like a child's ragdoll. Her heart was beating fast in her chest and her system was so pumped full of adrenalin she thought by sheer will alone she could wish herself to fly away.

But as she tried to rise, she then dropped back down. Her body was too badly bruised and in shock. She knew she would recover in time, would be able to get up, but as the creatures approached, she knew that time wouldn't be hers.

Resting her head on the grass, she gazed up at the sun and awaited her fate, praying it would be quick.

PART SIX

FINALE

Laura was shaking as she waited for the end to come, whether by razor sharp claws, by club, or by just being ripped apart.

She didn't have long to wait.

Less than thirty seconds after she was knocked to the ground, she saw the shadows of the creatures flow over her. They surrounded her. Four, eight foot tall monsters, with hair covering every inch of their bodies.

As she waited for the killing blow, she couldn't help but admire them. Muscles rippled beneath the coarse hair, and though their faces were far from looking human, there was a beautifulness to them.

One of the creatures planted its feet on either side of her, and it woofed a few times, as if it was talking to the others. The other three began to snarl, as if goading the one over her on.

Though she couldn't be sure, as the last survivor of the hunting party, she felt they were relishing her helplessness as they prepared to kill her.

She cringed in fear as the creature's right arm was raised, its claws glinting in the sun.

She closed her eyes and waited to feel those claws sink into her flesh, to tear out her heart like she was nothing but an animal brought down after a hunt.

Seconds passed and the killing blow didn't come, and though she couldn't believe she was thinking it, she wondered why she wasn't dead yet.

Opening her eyes, she saw the creature over her was looking down at her, its head cocked to the side as if it was curious about something.

And then she realized it wasn't looking at her, it was looking at the pendant hanging from her neck, the one her uncle had given her so many years ago.

Slowly, ever so slowly, she reached down and picked up the pendant, holding it a few inches from her chest so the creature could see it more clearly.

"You like this?" she said, her voice hoarse from all that she'd been through.

And then the creature did something she never would have expected. It stepped off her and knelt down beside her, then leaned over so its face was only a foot from hers.

A clawed hand reached out and touched the pendant, and when it did, the rock began to glow and suddenly, Laura heard a voice in her head, one that wasn't hers.

"DO NOT BE AFRAID. WE WILL NOT HARM YOU. YOU HAVE ONE OF THE STONES." She knew instantly it was the creature before her, and though it wasn't actually speaking, she could hear it clearly. It was as if the voice was in the center of her mind and had simply become there, instead of by way of her ears.

It was...telepathy!

What's happening? she wondered. *How can this be? It's impossible!*

She grew scared, her heart beating faster than even before when she thought she was about to be killed.

"FRIENDSHIP!" The word hit her like a bomb had gone off in her brain and she squeezed her eyes closed in pain. Her hands went to her ears as if she could stop the loud noise.

"WE ARE SORRY, WE KNOW NOT THE STRENGTH OF OUR MINDS," the voice said. "WE ARE USED TO ONLY TALKING TO OUR OWN KIND. WE HAVE NEVER TALKED TO HUMANS BEFORE. WE NEED TO ADJUST SO AS NOT TO FRIGHTEN YOU OR CAUSE YOU PAIN."

Laura lowered her hands from her ears and opened her eyes. She looked at the creatures with new eyes now, one that could sense they were not killers, but were in fact kind beings. Waves of love filled her and she knew many things about these beasts of the forest, their past flooding into her mind like a downloaded book.

How they had lived for centuries, hidden from man, and only wished to live in peace. But man was always encroaching on their home and each time the creatures would retreat to new, more remote locations.

They had become nomadic, and only stayed in one place when they knew it was entirely safe. Such as in the Adirondack Mountains, where acres of land remained untouched. They had settled in the mountains more than fifty years go and had lived quiet lives, being one with the forest.

All this flooded Laura's mind at the same time as her thoughts also went into the creatures' minds. As she learned of them, they too learned that Laura wasn't like the other hunters killed on the glade, that she was kind, and felt no joy in hunting down another animal of the forest, which at the time was what she believed to be a rogue grizzly bear.

"Then if that's true and you're peaceful, how do you explain what you did back at the cabin where two people were mauled and torn apart?" Laura asked.

"YOU DO NOT NEED TO SPEAK, MERELY THINK IT AND WE WILL HEAR YOU," the voice said. "WE CAN HEAR YOUR THOUGHTS BY WAY OF THE STONE. JUST FOCUS THEM AND WE WILL UNDERSTAND YOU."

"Okay, fine, but then why did you kill those people? And what about all my friends? You killed John."

"THOSE PEOPLE AT THE WOODEN STRUCTURE WERE KILLED OUT OF JUSTICE. THEY TOOK ONE OF OUR YOUNG, KILLED THE CHILD. WE HAD TO GET HIM BACK. WE TRIED TO MERELY TAKE OUR CHILD BUT THEY SHOT AT US, HURT US. SO WE RETURNED AGAIN IN THE NIGHT AND ATTACKED IN FORCE. THE PEOPLE RECEIVED JUSTICE BY OUR LAW. IF YOU KILL SO SHALL YOU BE KILLED."

"I see. An eye for an eye. We have something similar in our own laws."

"YES. AND I ASK YOU: WHAT WOULD YOU DO IF YOUR OFFSPRING WAS TAKEN IN THE NIGHT? WOULD YOU NOT DO EVERYTHING IN YOUR POWER TO RETRIEVE HIM?"

"Yes, I suppose I would. So then why did you kill my friends?"

"WE DID NOT WISH TO HURT THEM BUT WHAT WERE WE TO DO? YOU WERE HUNTING US, WISHED TO KILL US. WE DID WHAT WE BELIEVED TO BE RIGHT, WE PROTECTED OURSELVES, OUR LOVED ONES FROM DISCOVERY. IF NOT FOR THE STONE YOU WEAR, YOU TOO WOULD BE DEAD. BUT WE CAN SEE YOU ARE MORE LIKE US THAN THE HUMANS YOU TRAVELED WITH."

"Then you aren't going to kill me?"

"NO, WE WILL SPARE YOU. WE CAN READ YOUR THOUGHTS. WE KNOW YOU WILL NOT TELL OTHERS OF OUR EXISTENCE. YOU UNDERSTAND WE DID NOT KILL FOR ENJOYMENT BUT FOR SURVIVAL."

"But not all humans would want to harm you. Some would welcome knowing you exist."

"PERHAPS, BUT WE HAVE LIVED OUTSIDE THE HUMANS FOR A LONG TIME, WATCHING THEM, AND WE KNOW THEIR WAYS AND WE KNOW HOW EVIL THEY CAN BE." The creature leaned forward so its face was only a few inches from Laura's. "WE KNOW MANY THINGS, SOME BEYOND YOUR COMPREHENSION. WE ARE WISE IN THE WAYS OF THE EARTH. WE HAVE WATCHED HUMANS GROW FROM SMALL BEINGS WITH CLUBS AND STICKS FOR WEAPONS TO EVEN

ANTHONY GIANGREGORIO

SMALLER BEINGS WHO USE WEAPONS THAT SHOOT IRON FROM AFAR. WE KNOW OF THE COUNTLESS WARS SEEN THROUGH MOTHER EARTH AND WE KNOW THE HUMANS WILL NEVER STOP. THIS IS THEIR NATURE, IT CANNOT BE CHANGED. ALL WE CAN DO IS LIVE IN SECRECY AND STAY OUT OF THE PATH OF MAN."

"I understand, and I promise you I will never tell a soul about you. Your secret is safe with me."

"WE KNOW THIS OR WE WOULD NOT LET YOU LIVE. NOW, WE MUST GO. WAIT FOR US TO LEAVE AND THEN GO. DO WHAT YOU WILL WITH YOUR DEAD. BUT KNOW IF YOU LEAVE THEM, BY TONIGHT ALL SIGNS OF ANYTHING HAPPENING ON THIS GLADE WILL HAVE BEEN ERASED."

"I understand. And thank you."

"GO WITH MOTHER EARTH AS YOUR GUIDE. AND BE SAFE, LAURA CARSON."

She was about to ask how the creature could know her name but then realized it would be obvious if they could read her mind.

The creature stood up and as one they all turned and walked away. They paused only long enough to gather the bodies of their dead and wounded, and carrying their burdens, they lumbered back into the forest, leaving Laura where she had fallen, her eyes wide, her mouth open in amazement at what had just happened.

"FAREWELL," she heard once in her head and then the link was broken. She knew this for there had been a slight pressure in

142

her mind, and only with it gone did she realize it had been there in the first place.

She lay on the ground, not moving, for another ten minutes, her body slowly recovering from its ordeal. Then slowly, she sat up, and when she was confident she wouldn't fall back down, she tried to stand.

She felt dizzy for a moment but it passed quickly. Her side was throbbing but she could breathe well enough and knew, though she needed medical attention when she returned back to civilization, she would live past this day.

As she took in the carnage around her, she began to walk slowly, averting her gaze from the mauled bodies of her fellow Forest Rangers.

She found all the backpacks and rifled through them for the SAT phone, trying her best to ignore the gore covering the packs. When she found the phone, she discovered it was broken beyond repair. So much for calling in a chopper to take her home, she thought. It looked like she would be leaving the same way she came in.

She gathered what food and ammunition she could and made a small pile, then sat down and cried. She cried for all her friends dying needlessly, she cried for the death of Morrison, who she had really liked and thought it was very possible they could have had something special, something that could have lasted a lifetime, but now it was all gone.

As dusk began to set she decided it was time to leave. There was nothing she could do with the bodies of her fellow rangers so she had no choice but to leave them where they lay. After the connection she had with the creatures, she knew what the creatures said was true. By tomorrow morning, the bodies would be gone.

She would have no choice but to make camp somewhere on the hike home, but after what she'd just been through, sleeping alone in the forest was the least of her fears.

Her wounded ribs didn't allow her to carry much but she took what she could, concentrating on taking food and water mostly, then she began to walk to the edge of the large boulder where she would begin her climb back down.

It was as she was sitting on the edge of the large rock wall and about to begin her descent that she heard a voice calling out. At first she wondered if it was in her head, perhaps a residual effect of the stone pendant. She looked down to see if it was glowing like before but it wasn't.

Then the faint voice called out again, a distinctive, "Hello, is anyone up there! Help, I'm trapped!"

"John? Oh my God, it can't be!" she called out and ran as fast as she could to the edge of the drop-off.

When she reached the edge, she peered over it carefully, not wanting to fall off. Bitter irony that would be; to survive an attack by a clan of what could only have been called Bigfoots, to then fall off a cliff to her death.

As she leaned over ever so carefully, she was shocked and happy all at the same time to see Morrison's face looking up at her. His clothes were covered in dirt and were torn in a few places and he had a good-sized gash on his forehead that had bled profusely but had now stopped.

"Hey there," he said with a smile. "Thank God you heard me. Would you mind tossing me down a rope or something, please? I can't get up on my own."

She studied the side of the drop-off and saw it was solid rock with almost no indentations where a climber could grab on to. If she had been killed by the creatures, John would have starved to death on the little outcropping he'd been lucky enough to land on.

She smiled as wide as possible as tears filled her eyes in relief. John was alive! She wasn't alone!

"Hang on, I'll toss a rope down to you!" she called and began doing just that. She tied one end to a nearby tree and dropped the rest down. A few minutes later, with some huffing and puffing, John's head appeared at the edge of the drop-off, then his shoulders.

He slid his right knee over the edge and pulled himself up with his hands. Laura was there to help him but she couldn't do much because of her ribs.

When he was back on solid ground, he laid down and sucked in air, glad to be free of his elevated prison.

She hugged and kissed him, crying uncontrollably. She was never much of a crier but she felt it was warranted now. "I can't believe you're alive," she wept.

"Hey, it'll take a lot more than a bunch of giant hairy monsters and a cliff to stop me," he joked, trying to be macho though not feeling it. He had never felt so helpless than when he was on that outcropping with nothing but a drop to his death if he decided he couldn't stand starving to death.

"I guess so," she laughed as she hugged him harder.

Morrison gently released her and looked around the glade, not seeing anyone else, the mangled bodies of the other Rangers hidden in the tall grass, but remembering when he had watched some of the other Rangers killed and the explosion of Bill's hand grenade. "Are we the only ones who made it? Where are those things, did we scare them off?"

Laura couldn't help but smile at his questions. "No, it's only the two of us left. And yes, the creatures have left."

"How did you survive?" he asked. "Did you hide?"

"No, not exactly," she said and pulled him towards the large rock wall, only pausing to untie the rope from the tree as they walked. They would need it for their descent down the boulder. "But I think I might have a broken rib or two."

"Really? How did that happen, and how did you manage to avoid getting killed?" He paused and then said, "Not that I'm complaining, mind you." He hugged her again and kissed her passionately. "When I came to, one of the things that drove me crazy when I was down on that ledge was wondering if you were alive or dead. I couldn't bear to think you were dead. I guess I got knocked out when I landed and when I came to I checked my watch to see that I'd been out for almost an hour."

"How I survived is a long story, and one I hope you'll believe when I tell it to you. But listen, what happened here, those creatures we found, we can't tell anyone what happened. We have to keep them a secret."

He looked surprised and confused. "What? But why? Those creatures were unbelievable, they shouldn't exist, whatever they are. It'll be on all the news channels, we'll be famous! And if we keep it a secret, then how the hell are we gonna explain what happened to the other people on our team? If everyone's dead, there's gonna be an inquiry, questions asked, we'll have to explain it all to everyone's satisfaction."

"And we will, we'll have plenty of time on our way home to figure out what we can say. The Adirondack is massive, we can say we got separated and never saw them again. It happens all the time, people go missing and are never found, even groups that are camping. Flash floods, rock slides, this is a dangerous place, despite its beauty. But you have to trust me when I say I have a damn good reason why those creatures and what happened here must stay a secret."

"Well, I trust you but I have the right to change my mind until I've heard your reasons why."

"Fair enough," she said, knowing once he heard the whole story he would understand. She sat him down on the ledge and reached for the first aid kit. "Now let's get you cleaned up so we can leave. Believe me when I say we don't want to be here when night falls."

"Okay, but I have another question."

"Yes?"

"Those ribs you hurt, does that mean when we get back to my hotel room there won't be a repeat of last night." He was smirking now.

She laughed, strong and hard, the feeling of joy filling her with happiness. "We'll see, loverboy, but let's get back there first, then we'll see whether it'll be slow or fast."

"Slow or fast, huh? Then that's a yes?"

When she had cleaned his wound, she placed a bandage on his forehead and slapped his shoulder. "We'll see," she smiled, knowing it most definitely was a yes.

Morrison tied off the rope and she told him to go down first, then he could hold the rope taut for her to climb down.

She dropped the backpacks down to him and he caught them— now two more than before with Morrison carrying them— and prepared to climb down herself.

When her legs were over the edge and she was about to duck down, she felt a pressure in her mind again and the pendant around her neck began to glow. She knew what was happening immediately. Across the glade, her eyes began scanning the treeline for a few seconds, then one of the creatures was there, seeming to appear as if out of thin air.

"BE SAFE, LAURA CARSON. WE ARE GLAD YOUR MATE IS STILL ALIVE," the voice said, then the creature blended back into the treeline, gone from her sight no matter how hard she tried to see where it went.

"You also, and don't worry. John will keep your secret, too, I promise," she thought, but don't know if the creature was still there to hear her.

"Come on, slow poke, it's gonna be dark soon!" Morrison called up to her.

"Coming!" she replied, and with one last look at the treeline, a part of her wishing the creature would still be there, she began the descent down the boulder, and back to civilization.

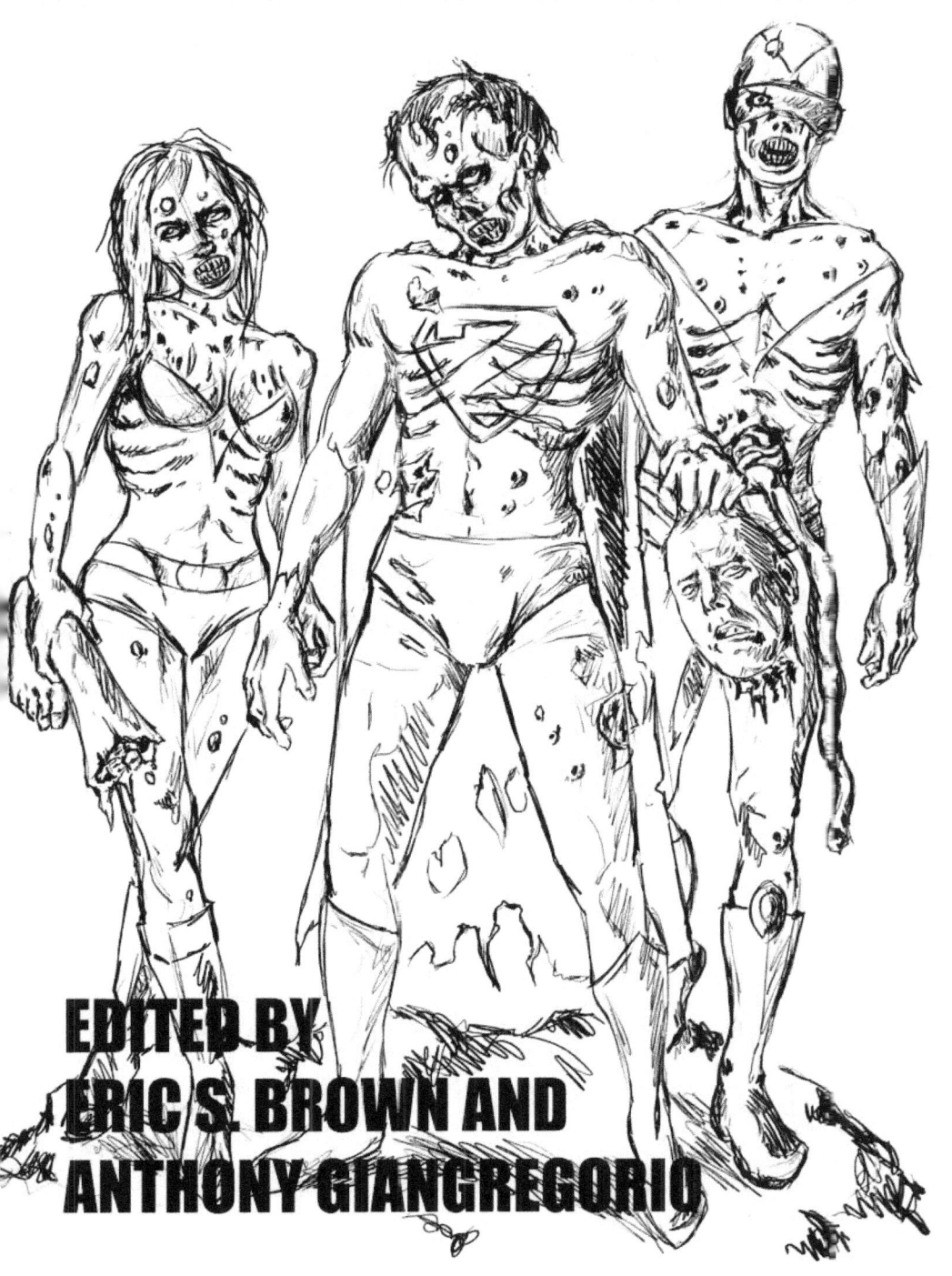

SUPERHEROES VS. ZOMBIES

EDITED BY
ERIC S. BROWN AND
ANTHONY GIANGREGORIO

THE WAR AGAINST THEM: A ZOMBIE NOVEL
by Jose Alfredo Vazquez

Mankind wasn't prepared for the onslaught.

An ancient organism is reanimating the dead bodies of its victims, creating worldwide chaos and panic as the disease spreads to every corner of the globe. As governments struggle to contain the disease, courageous individuals across the planet learn what it truly means to make choices as they struggle to survive.

Geopolitics meet technology in a race to save mankind from the worst threat it has ever faced. Doctors, military and soldiers from all walks of life battle to find a cure. For the dead walk, and if not stopped, they will wipe out all life on Earth. Humanity is fighting a war they cannot win, for who can overcome Death itself? Man versus the walking dead with the winner ruling the planet. Welcome to *The War Against Them*.

THE TURNING: A STORY OF THE LIVING DEAD
by Kelly M. Hudson

The Dead Walk!

And no place on earth is safe from their ravening hunger. Civilization falls, leaving groups of struggling survivors to navigate a world that has descended into Hell.

Jeff Richards is one such survivor. He and his lover Jenny flee their home in the Bay Area and take a perilous journey through Northern California into Oregon, seeking shelter in rural areas to avoid both the living dead and that most treacherous animal of all: their fellow humans.

But can a man who has lost everything, including his humanity, ever be reborn?

When the dead walk, will any of us survive?

Or will we all join the ranks of the undead to forever walk the earth.

END OF DAYS: AN APOCALYPTIC ANTHOLOGY
VOLUMES 1-3

Edited by Anthony Giangregorio

Our world is a fragile place.

Meteors, famine, floods, nuclear war, solar flares, and hundreds of other calamities can plunge our small blue planet into turmoil in an instant.

What would you do if tomorrow the sun went super nova or the world was swallowed by water, submerging the world into the cold darkness of the ocean? This anthology explores some of those scenarios and plunges you into total annihilation.

But remember, it's only a book, and tomorrow will come as it always does. Or will it?

KINGDOM OF THE DEAD
by Anthony Giangregorio
THE DEAD HAVE RISEN!

In the dead city of Pittsburgh, two small enclaves struggle to survive, eking out an existence of hand to mouth.

But instead of working together, both groups battle for the last remaining fuel and supplies of a city filled with the living dead.

Six months after the initial outbreak, a lone helicopter arrives bearing two more survivors and a newborn baby. One enclave welcomes them, while the other schemes to steal their helicopter and escape the decaying city.

With no police, fire, or social services existing, the two will battle for dominance in the steel city of the walking dead. But when the dust settles, the question is: will the remaining humans be the winners, or the losers?

When the dead walk, the line between Heaven and Hell is so twisted and bent there is no line at all.

RISE OF THE DEAD
by Anthony Giangregorio
DEATH IS ONLY THE BEGINNING!

In less than forty-eight hours, more than half the globe was infected.

In another forty-eight, the rest would be enveloped.

The reason?

A science experiment gone horribly wrong which enabled the dead to walk, their flesh rotting on their bones even as they seek human prey.

Jeremy was an ordinary nineteen year old slacker. He partied too much and had done poorly in high school. After a night of drinking and drugs, he awoke to find the world a very different place from the one he'd left the night before.

The dead were walking and feeding on the living, and as Jeremy stepped out into a world gone mad, the dead spotting him alone and unarmed in the middle of the street,

he had to wonder if he would live long enough to see his twentieth birthday.

THE CHRONICLES OF JACK PRIMUS
BOOK ONE
by Michael D. Griffiths

Beneath the world of normalcy we all live in lies another world, one where supernatural beings exist. These creatures of the night hunt us; want to feed on our very souls, though only a few know of their existence.

One such man is Jack Primus, who accidentally pierces the veil between this world and the next. With no other choice if he wants to live, he finds himself on the run, hunted by beings called the Xemmoni, an ancient race that sees humans as nothing but cattle. They want his soul, to feed on his very essence, and they will kill all who stand in their way. But if they thought Jack would just lie down and accept his fate, they were sorely mistaken. He didn't ask for this battle, but he knew he would fight them with everything at his disposal, for to lose is a fate worse than death.

He would win this war, and he would take down anyone who got in his way.

ETERNAL NIGHT: A VAMPIRE ANTHOLOGY
Edited by Anthony Giangregorio

Blood, fangs, darkness and terror...these are the calling cards of the vampire mythos.

Inside this tome are stories that embrace vampire history but seek to introduce a new literary spin on this longstanding fictional monster. Follow a dark journey through cigarette-smoking creatures hunted by rogue angels, vampires that feed off of thoughts instead of blood, immortals presenting the fantastic in a local rock band, to a legendary monster on the far reaches of town.

Forget what you know about vampires; this anthology will destroy historical mythos and embrace incredible new twists on this celebrated, fictional character.

Welcome to a world of the undead, welcome to the world of *Eternal Night*.

DEAD HISTORY 2
A Zombie Anthology

Edited by Anthony Giangregorio
From the dawn of mankind, the walking dead have been with us.

The greatest moments in history are not what they appear.

Through the ages, the undead have been there, only the proof has been erased, documents destroyed, and witnesses silenced.

The living dead is man's greatest secret.

In this tome, are a few of the stories of what really happened all those years ago. History isn't alive, it's dead!

INSIDE THE PERIMETER: SCAVENGERS OF THE DEAD
by Alan Spencer

In the middle of nowhere, the vestiges of an abandoned town are surrounded by inescapably high concrete barriers, permitting no trespass or escape. The town is dormant of human life, but rampant with the living dead, who choose not to eat flesh, but to instead continue their survival by cruder means.

Boyd Broman, a detective arrested and falsely imprisoned, has been transferred into the secret town. He is given an ultimatum: recapture Hayden Grubaugh, the cannibal serial killer, who has been banished to the town, in exchange for his freedom.

During Boyd's search, he discovers why the psychotic cannibal must really be captured and the sinister secrets the dead town holds.

With no chance of escape, Broman finds himself trapped among the ravenous, violent dead. With the cannibal feeding on the animated cadavers and the undead searching for Boyd, he must fulfill his end of the deal before the rotting corpses turn him into an unwilling organ donor.

But Boyd wasn't told that no one gets out alive, that the town is a death sentence. For there is no escape from *Inside the Perimeter*.

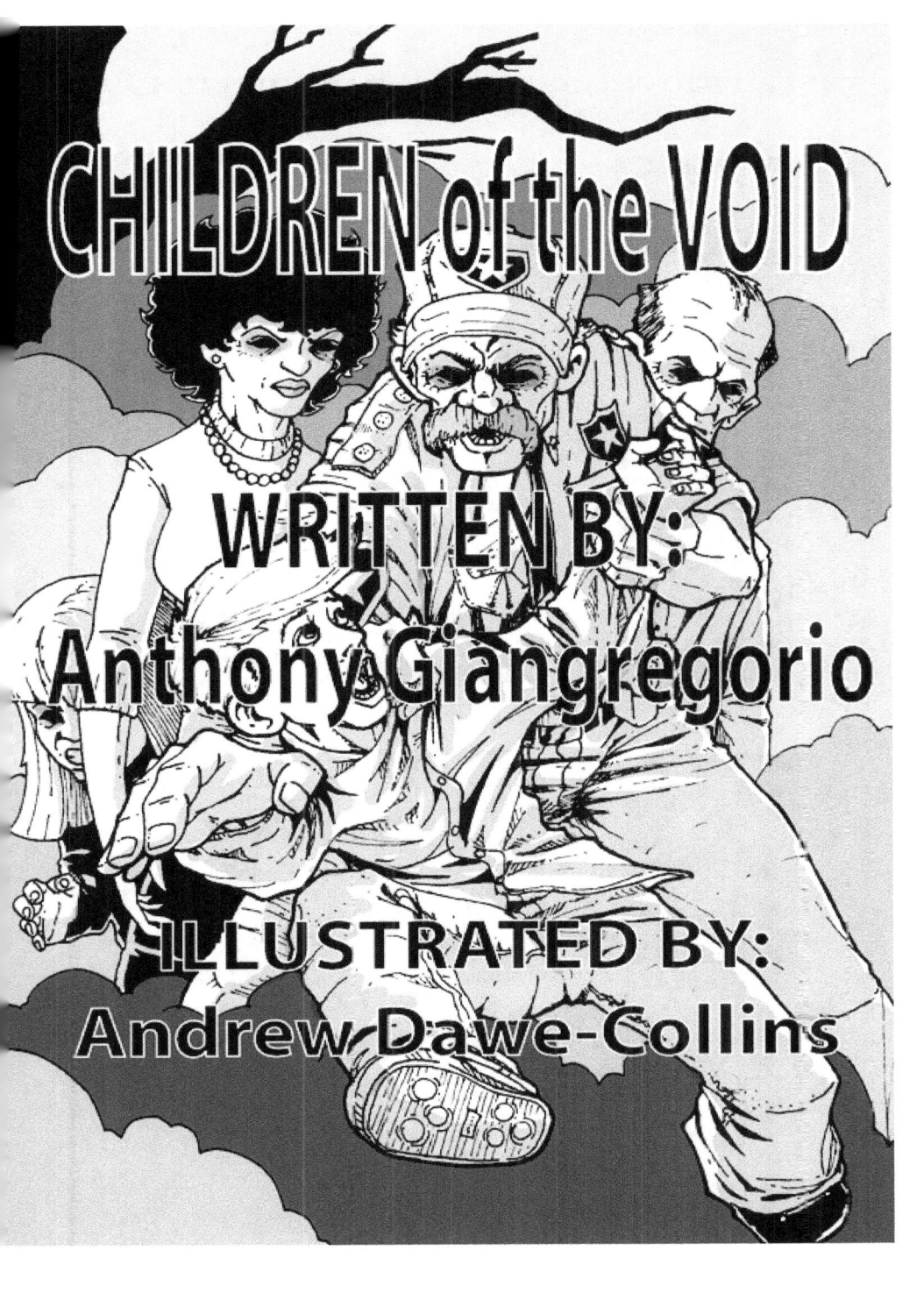

THE PLACE TO GO FOR ZOMBIE AND APOCALYPTIC FICTION

LIVING DEAD PRESS
WHERE THE DEAD WALK
www.livingdeadpress.com

www.ingramcontent.com/pod-product-compliance
Lightning Source LLC
Chambersburg PA
CBHW070959120726
47910CB00004B/1309